Clara Dupont‑Monod

THE REVOLT

Translated from the French by
Ruth Diver

Quercus

First published in the French language as *La révolte* by Editions Stock, Paris, in 2018
First published in Great Britain in 2020 by

Quercus Editions Ltd
Carmelite House
50 Victoria Embankment
London EC4Y 0DZ

An Hachette UK company

ROYAUME-UNI

This book is supported by the Institut français (Royaume-Uni) as part of the
Burgess programme.

A CIP catalogue record for this book is available
from the British Library

HB ISBN 978 1 52940 288 9
TPB ISBN 978 1 52940 289 6

10 9 8 7 6 5 4 3 2 1

Typeset by Jouve (UK), Milton Keynes

Printed and bound in Great Britain by Clays Ltd, Elcograf S.p.A.

"Your spirit is like a storm-beaten wall.
You look around you and cannot find rest."

Letter by Hildegard of Bingen
to Eleanor of Aquitaine, twelfth century

IN MY MOTHER'S EYES, I see things that overwhelm me. I see vast conquests, deserted houses, and suits of armour. She carries a rage within herself that condemns me, and forces me to be a better man.

This evening, she comes to us. Her gown caresses the floor. At this moment, we are like the stones in the vaulted ceiling, immobile and breathless. But what petrifies my brothers is not her indifference, for they are used to being ignored, nor the solemnity of the meeting – everything about Eleanor is solemn – no, what transfixes us, at this moment, is her voice. For it is with a soft voice, full of menace, that my mother commands us to overthrow our father.

She says that she has raised us for this task. That she made sure we grew up here, in Aquitaine, and not in England, so she could teach us the nobility of her lineage. Indeed, is my name not Richard the Lionheart? The time has come for us to assert ourselves. She reminds us that she asked troubadours to sing legends at our births. One for each child. She tells us that here, where we now stand, where we learned to walk, in this great hall of the palace of Poitiers, the spirit of our great-grandfather is breathing his strength into us. You have heard his poems, she says, and the stories of his exploits. And so, my sons, you are armed. You are fourteen, fifteen, and sixteen years old. The time has come.

We know these words. They flow through our veins. Henry, Geoffrey, and I will obey, each for our own reasons. But we are bound together by one certainty: Eleanor can be threatened, she can be defied, and even fought. But betrayed, never. And maybe my father knew this, in fact. Maybe he wanted to wound his wife in her very heart. That idea turns our countries to ice. For in that case, what we must now engage in is not a matter of personal revenge, but the clash of two monsters ready to fight to the death. And we, their children, will be mere toys between their paws.

My mother is a self-assured woman. I have absolute faith in her. She owes this assurance to her birth, for she is the Duchess of Aquitaine, raised amid luxury and learning, haloed by the memory of her grandfather, the first poet. For her there is no difference between silk and sapience. She managed her fiefs with an iron hand from the very start. Vassals' rebellions, harvests, defining borders, settling disputes . . . Eleanor likes to rule, and she knows every alleyway of even the smallest village of her Aquitaine. For she carries her land like a jewel melted into her skin. A powerful jewel: Aquitaine is an immense and wealthy territory, stretching from Poitou to the Spanish border and spilling into Limousin and the Auvergne. The lord of such a land is far more powerful than the king of France. I know that this might seem strange, but in this era that is mine, a nobleman can have greater power than a monarch, if his lands are vaster. That is why the king of France, Louis VII, had to marry Eleanor. She was presented to him. And he fell madly in love with her.

He was fifteen years old, she was thirteen. He had a pure heart, but purity never held much sway with Eleanor. For fifteen years she was queen of France, and very bored. She did not give Louis an heir. She loved literature, he loved the Gospels; she called for feasting and wars, he wished for peace and conversation. She believes in power, he in God.

She managed to have her marriage with Louis annulled – something that a queen never does, ever, any more than a wife launches an offensive against her husband. But that is how it is, my mother is a trailblazer. These are not the words of an adoring child, no, her decisions and actions have no model, no precedent, and ultimately, I believe that this series of "firsts" betrays her long-held yearning for innocence.

After her departure, she set her sights on a man eleven years her junior, Henry Plantagenet. He needed her Aquitaine, the size of a whole country. He became king of England, and my mother was a queen again. This time she had many children, including Henry, Geoffrey, and me.

The outline of their story looks like a beautiful stained-glass window. A blazing royal couple, at the head of an empire that covers England and Aquitaine, surrounded by valiant heirs . . . Balanced in their presence, with my father most often in England, my mother in Aquitaine, and us, their children, quite used to travelling back and forth between them. But also, a flaw. Invisible on the official image, but so deep that it engulfed violence, spite, and hatred.

For my mother thought that she would retain her suzerainty over Aquitaine. That was her marriage contract with my father: she brought him her lands, whose expanse carried real power; in return, he would protect her autonomy, would not interfere in her rule over her domains, and would even, since she loved power so much, involve her in the rule of England. It was a fair exchange. But in the end, these two exceptional beings were not spared the banal fate of ordinary mortals: first being betrayed, and then seeking revenge.

Carried by her assurance, and by the certainty that she would make the best of her destiny, my mother believed she was marrying a harmless creature. But very quickly, the Plantagenet confiscated everything. He treated Aquitaine as he later treated England, like a conquered realm. He changed everything according to his wishes – its coinage, justice, and language, its laws of trade and fishing, the boundaries of the forests – and ignored the rising dissent. The lords of Aquitaine detested him immediately. My father paid them no heed. He revealed himself to be authoritarian, despotic, greedy. My mother was nothing but a belly, swelling almost every year.

Understanding her mistake, my mother set her hopes on

the coronation of her eldest son, named Henry like his father. She thought she could rule a little through him, recover her full rights. Many monarchs around us are now in the habit of crowning a son in order to assure the continuity of their dynasty. They initiate him in the exercise of power, legitimise him in the eyes of the people. This happens through a mutual understanding between fathers and sons. The Plantagenet played along and duly crowned Henry . . . but now ignores his presence. This is another of his betrayals. He remains the sole master. He refuses to relinquish anything. He belongs to that strange race of men who are always in company, yet always alone. He has heard neither the anger of the dispossessed barons nor our own. He wants everyone to be subjugated to his will, starting of course with Aquitaine, which my mother brought to him by marriage. The Plantagenet is refashioning the whole world to his glory. But that world includes Eleanor.

Today, revenge occupies my mother completely. Ever since she announced the revolt against the Plantagenet, she has been pacing up and down the great hall of Poitiers, marching like a general before her armies. Her long leather belt bounces against her gown. She masters several languages, and I see messengers come and go from distant lands, the emissaries, the allies of the last hour. Coffers full of coins are set at her feet and testers bite them to make sure they are real gold. Voices are lowered. The poets dare not rehearse in their chambers.

I chance upon my mother at sunrise, standing before the table in the great hall. The morning stretches its ropes of light through the windows. Eleanor stands between two powdery rays suspended between the floor and the ceiling, which seem to follow the lines my mother is drawing on a map. Here is my father's empire, from the North Sea to the Pyrenees. There is no one more powerful than he.

Eleanor's bracelets clink against the wood. She counts the rallying points, calculates the distances. I see her slim wrists sheathed in silk, the curve of the veil covering her chignon and tumbling down her back. And then a memory rises up. I see that same profile bent over our cradles. From that silhouette came a story belonging to each one of us. Its melody would reach the rafters of the halls and the depths of the valleys of Aquitaine, blending snowy days and Saint John's Eve, lullabies and battle songs. The years have passed, but those softly sung stories have stayed with us, hanging in our hearts like talismans, made of her voice, her image, the face I am observing this morning, which still has the same worried brow, the same long pointy eyelashes.

My mother does not know that I am observing her. She is a one-woman offensive, her body tense, leaning forward, concentrating entirely on the attack. As children, we already knew her love only as a concentrated force ready to pounce, and this soothed us.

She straightens up. I almost flinch. As usual, I feel a mixture of terror and strength engulf me. She beckons me over, and I know what she will say. When she speaks to me, it will only be to consider the day of the battle. She will talk to me of my father. He has been her obsession, has fuelled her hatred, for many years now. During their official appearances, in spite of the court and the crowds, she would only ever look at him, the Plantagenet. Her wide grey eyes no longer even saw me. And I feel ashamed of this, but sometimes I wish she hated me too.

There's no point waiting for words of love. My mother has never pronounced any. This does not sadden me. My era is miserly with words. It respects them too much to shower them on crowds, to use them every which way. A day will surely come when everyone will talk so much that they will no longer say anything at all. But here and now, words are still an act of engagement. They are so prized that they determine life or death. The knight respects the word he gives to his lady, even if it costs him his life; the lord obeys his oath; war and peace are decided by a single sentence. One must keep one's word. And so Eleanor never says any tender words to us. She understands their value too well to squander them. My mother hardly ever lowers her guard. She always stays on the edges of her true self, wary, tense, and invites no one inside her.

She has other ways of speaking. I have discovered that she ensures that the apothecary monk is present at each of my training sessions. He prepares his sage balm, verbena poultices, burdock unguent, and other fast-acting remedies, in case I am injured. For my sisters, my mother has ribbons brought all the way from Baghdad, of chiffon so light it melts into their hair. My brother is organising a hunt? He will find a new saddle, of fresh leather, made for him overnight. This is my mother's tenderness, expressed not with words, but hidden gestures.

Her greatest declaration was indeed a gesture. She offered me her Aquitaine. Aware of my father's threat weighing upon it, Eleanor gave her land to me. Mine to defend and to honour. I was fourteen years old. I entered the church of Saint Hilary in Poitiers, shielded by the arches with their white arms. The bishop handed me the sword, slipped the ring onto my finger, and attached my spurs. I became the Duke of Aquitaine. I pronounced the oath on my knees, in a strong voice: "Raise up what has been destroyed, preserve what is standing." I felt an immense happiness. This was the order of things, and I was taking my place within it, the one my mother had offered me.

Then she told me of her kingdom. She wanted to stress its difference from England, "the cradle of your birth, Richard, but a land without a soul, full of rain and misery. No one knows how to read over there."

In Aquitaine, the dead rise up on the pathways, and fountains can boil while remaining cold. I learned these beliefs. We wear a marsh stone as a necklace. We have to eat fruit under its tree, as a simple way of thanking the tree. The Church may well have marked out the entire country, but for the local people, the colour of the sky has as much value as a sermon. We love nature to the point of being able to read it. Now I know how to look at a linden tree's bark, to see when the bast is ready to be extracted to make rope for the wells. I recognise the sounds of the different bells, all of which have names. Attacking a neighbour, or even royalty, is a daily hobby: Aquitanians have revolt in their blood. I have quashed all those who contested Eleanor's authority – since all I know how to do is to make war. I have stamped her seal with the naïve pride of children who know they are chosen.

And of all this colour, nothing remains but a battle plan.

Sometimes I manage to stand back, to dissect the disaster. I ask myself, can anyone survive the decision to kill their own father? And why did mine place so much importance on his own desires at the expense of ours? What interest did he have in setting the family against him? For here it is, the irony of it all: hatred brings the family together. Up until now, my elder brother and I had very little in common. I was the impulsive one, and Henry, the haughty one . . . I cared only for strumpets, fighting, solitude. He intends to marry a princess, prefers discussions to weapons and adores parading about with his court . . . One detail summarises all of our differences: I love hunting boar, Henry despises it. He prefers the stag, the animal of kings. But while the boar might be dirty and ugly, with its crooked little trotters, you still have to fight it body to body, breath to breath. It might be brought to bay by the dogs, but the final attack happens on the ground, as equals. You will never see a boar refusing to fight, unlike the cowardly stag, which gives up and lets itself be killed. Every time I've brought a boar back from the hunt, Henry has refused to eat its meat.

Sustained by the certainty of someday acceding to the throne, he always looked down on me, as if violence were dirty. My mother, conscious of our differences, took the initiative. She arranged for me to be raised alongside another boy, a colossus named Mercadier. I've seen him dodge the furious attack of a boar a dozen times . . . Small, close-set eyes that seem to float in a wide face, an enormous jaw, long matted hair and hands the size of laundry paddles, Mercadier is a creature from a fairy tale who reconciles me with humanity. He was an abandoned child, found as a baby, wrapped in a straw cocoon, on the steps of the palace of Poitiers. My mother saw this as a sign of destiny. She gambled on his size and cheery disposition, and was proven right. Mercadier is the brother I always dreamed of having. He has always been right behind me, vigilant, mischievous, a battler like no one else. His gratitude guarantees his loyalty. With him, I've known companionship and affection. It was good for me. I had Mercadier, as valorous and faithful as Henry can be scornful and frivolous.

I have a memory of my brother one Christmas Eve, in England. We were about ten years old. The castle was lit up with candles. The shadows stretched in fluid forms that crawled up the walls as the court paraded slowly past to pay homage to us. My father, who detests ceremonies, accepted the lords' bows, while wondering which of them he would attack first. Henry was immobile, standing stiffly in his gold-striped tunic, a sham little sovereign, glancing at my father from time to time to take deportment lessons. It was endearing and pathetic at the same time. Henry looked downwards; my father stood perfectly straight. He was arrogant; my father was self-assured. Before my eyes were all the differences between domination and rule, and I quickly turned away, looking for the form of Mercadier, who stood in a pool of shadow, bored out of his wits.

But since then, now that we are in league against my father, Henry and I have become closer. Now, he suggests weapons, discusses manoeuvres, asks for my advice. He no longer judges me. I can feel the fear hidden under his regal poise. I've had many chances to confirm the fact that there is no one more dangerous than a humiliated man. It was my mother's advice: "Kill, or spare a life. But do not wound. A wounded man becomes a dangerous animal."

For while I have Aquitaine, my brother possesses nothing. He was anointed king of England, he married a princess, and . . . he cannot govern. My father will not cede a thing to him. He is the laughing stock of Europe. The taverns and ports are filled with songs mocking him. How can he be credible when his crown is no more than a toy? My father deprives him not only of power, but also of respect. And so for years, Henry has kept his distance and stewed in his spite. He held his own court at Bonneville-sur-Touques, in Normandy. Well, I say a court . . . more like an orgy. He had no personal income, since my father refuses to give him one, so he pilfered from the royal coffers. Of course, the courtiers swarmed around him and enjoyed the lavish banquets, but my mother had to call him to order and summon him back to Poitiers. She has long known how to recognise sadness disguised as insolence.

Years ago, I surprised Henry crouching at the edge of a pond, busy covering his head with mud. Of all of us, he is the one who looks most like our father with his square face, red hair, and fine lips sealed in a bitter sneer. Kneeling at the water's edge, he was scooping up big brown handfuls of slime. It spread over his skull, falling in clumps on his shoulders. He was grunting like a piglet. I didn't tarry there.

But I must be honest. Despite the new closeness forged by the revolt, we siblings remain solitary beings. There are seven of us. Seven frontiers to cross. I feel closest to Matilda, my eldest sister, but I do not know her well. We were suspicious of each other as we were growing up, waiting for a sign from our father. None of us ever got one, except the youngest of us all: John, who arrived almost like an intruder, one Christmas Eve in the icy palace at Oxford. My mother was in her forties. And then there were four sons. Against all expectations, my father immediately took to him. He even wrapped the baby's head in a bandage to save him from bumping it! No one had ever seen the Plantagenet take such care of a child. John was the little king, which was why we hated him.

We should have grown up holding each other close. Henry would have taught me how to look after the finances, I would have helped Geoffrey polish his dagger, held up mirrors for my sisters. Especially for Matilda, born one year before me, Matilda with her straight back and pale wrists, so similar to my mother. Matilda, who had leaned over me and pressed her hands to my ears one evening, so I wouldn't hear the deafening noise of thunder — as a child I wanted to go into battle against the storm. She knew of my sudden bursts of rage and whispered my birth song. I breathed in the smell of her hair and recognised the scent of lilies. My mother used to cover the floors of our bedchambers with them.

The Plantagenet gave us nothing, except his respect for the sword. The sword betrays no one, that is why it is my only friend. The idea that we would one day take up my father's role floated above our heads, and yet we hardly knew his face. We felt the hatred that was rising against him. The great barons of Aquitaine bustled around my mother, whispering amongst themselves. The lords paraded at court, clamouring to be received immediately by the king, who had redrawn the boundaries of their domains. But the king was not there. He was always on the roads, roaming through his kingdom to bring it to heel. We, his sons, were expected to be worthy of an absent model, to take our lead from a ghost. In that great fog whose shape was the future, my mother was a beacon. Her status as queen obliged us to change residences often – Eng-land or France, Caen, Niort, Falaise, Poitiers – but she always took us with her. She watched over us.

Not a single tender word, as I said, and never any gentle caresses either. From very early on, we felt that for our mother, happiness always went hand in hand with a threat. If she never embraced her children, it was because she feared their loss. She can sense where danger is hiding, the threat that those she cherishes will be taken from her. That is what dam-aged souls are like. But love betrays itself anyway. One day, I asked my mother why she never attended my weapons train-ing, since I excelled at it and I knew how highly she valued warriors. She raised her hand and, intuitively, I lowered my brow. I needn't have bothered. She said, "I can bear the sight of anything, except your blood." All of Eleanor is there, in suspended tenderness, in promises hidden under evasion. I would like to embrace her, but of course I do no such thing. I content myself with listening to those mute declarations com-ing from her suspicious heart, and they are what now gives me the strength to tell this history.

Before the Revolt

APRIL 1152. FIFTEEN YEARS AGO. A feast day. The Poitevins form a circle in the town square. Their voices rise, full of joy, as they start the first verse.

> *At the dawning of fair weather,*
> *To find joy again, and vex the jealous one,*
> *The queen wishes to show*
> *How she is in love . . .*

The chorus flows up to the towers then frolics through the alleyways, as graceful and light as the ribbons the girls tie around their waists. I can still hear the hands clapping to the rhythm of the song: "*Regina avrilloza! Regina avrilloza!*"

That "Queen of a day in April" is my mother.

She has just left the king of France.

At the markets, around the wells, in faraway places, carried by breathless messengers, commented on in royal council halls, spread throughout the monasteries, everywhere, the news breaks like a storm. The powerful purse their lips. But the people recognise the audacity of her act. They have always loved Eleanor. They drink to her health. They say that this month of April 1152 will be remembered as the time when a woman showed the meaning of skill. They imagine her galloping through the countryside, leaving a capital and a king behind her. And it's true. Eleanor has managed to have her marriage annulled, with the consent of the Church. She is abandoning Louis VII and her title as queen. No woman had ever dared to do so.

They whisper that Louis will not recover from this. He has spent his life shrivelled up in the hope that she might look at him. He has gone against his own convictions. And what carnage! For his wife, Louis the believer, Louis the pure burned innocent people, destroyed a crusade, stained his hands with black blood. And she leaves with the wind in her hair.

His advisors seek another wife for him in Spain, but Louis thinks only of my mother. He prays every day, they say, for no harm to come to her. And this, despite his jealousy, despite the lurking presence of that young man who has never ceased to defy him, the Plantagenet, the duke of Normandy and future king of England.

He had presented himself at court a few months earlier, had bowed to my mother. She had stiffened, suddenly alert. Her slight smile fooled no one.

Louis had understood everything. He hadn't even tried to argue with Eleanor. That night, he kept his eyes open. He listened to his wife's regular breathing. He thought about the man who would soon take his place. His defeat would bear the name of the common broom flower – *planta genista*. The Plantagenet was a squat mass, a lion's head, a fearsome warrior thirsting with ambition. The exact opposite of Louis, who was tall, slim and blond, with soft eyes.

Eleanor is galloping through the countryside, now single again. She is thinking about the Plantagenet. It's a little early to be remarried, she has only just left the king of France . . . But she foresees that he will go far. He is younger than her, but so what? He will become king of England, that's obvious to her. Her decision is made. She will marry him. He will accept, of course, since she will bring him her Aquitaine. The future looks happy. Eleanor is thirty years old and acts as she pleases. She is not worried. Louis will surely remarry as well. Her life is no longer tied to his. Her city of Poitiers awaits. Her men at arms accompany her – wherever she goes, I've always seen my mother surrounded by men. Louis never took well to this, whereas my father is indifferent.

In the yellow fields, the bent figures of the peasants rise up and bow to her. The carts make way as she passes. Eleanor rides like a man, something the Parisian court always held against her. Her chignon bumps against the back of her neck and slowly uncoils. Her cape billows in the wind, fastened by a golden brooch. She hums a song, something about sunshine and rebirth.

She wants to stop at Blois, where the town is preparing for Palm Sunday. This delights my mother. During her years of marriage to the pious Louis, her Aquitanian blood had nearly dried up. It was crying out for music, crowds, decorations in the streets. It was sick from the silence. But tomorrow, my mother will glide into the midst of the dancing circles and drink wine. She will try not to stumble among the animals, especially the pigs – my mother has a particular fondness for these animals, the first inhabitants of our towns and part of our daily lives. People love them to the point of claiming they have a soul, and sometimes judging them in courts of law. My mother loves all animals indiscriminately. She knows all the birds, takes care of her horse's comfort, and saves a part of any banquet for the dogs. Her favourite holiday is the Feast of the Ass, in the middle of winter, when the animal is led to the church altar, cloaked in a splendid garment, as the congregation brays ... Then it is taken out of church with great ceremony, and the crowd dances around it, ignoring the disapproval of the clergy, which only adds to my mother's enjoyment. She will see an ass again tomorrow, in Blois, pulled along the streets by a jubilant crowd of townsfolk. Their cheeks will be chafed by all the waving boughs, their mouths full of songs. I get my liking for inns, ruffians, and open bodices from my mother. People say I should marry. But I prefer the soft, sweet girls in the taverns, touched a thousand times, who hold out their goblets with a smile.

Eleanor is heading for the castle of Thibaut, the count of

Champagne. He sent her an invitation, affixed with a seal she finds terribly arrogant. She accepted, impatient to attend the feast, and plans to spend the night there.

Her cavalcade approaches the castle, but, suddenly, Eleanor freezes. There are too many armed men at the foot of the walls. She perceives tension, gathered forces waiting for a signal. Where will it come from? And why are all the soldiers carrying their shields? Emblazoned on them is the count's coat of arms, eight arrows arranged as a star. The top point leads Eleanor's eyes upwards. In the wall, a slit lights up. Someone has quickly stepped back from an arrow loop.

Eleanor slowly rides onto the drawbridge. She feels for the blade sewn into the lining at the side of her bodice. This is a trick she inherited from her grandfather. (I adopted it too, and perfected it. The blade springs up under pressure, so if an enemy throws their weight on top of me, it will pierce his heart.)

She stops her horse in the middle of the courtyard. She waits there, her thighs tight around its flanks, her waist straight, her chin slightly to one side. Her eyes inspect, search, pierce the shadows with their silver intensity. The falcons are out for the first April hunts. Soon the winter-born calves will be led outside. Everything seems welcoming except . . . Eleanor's eyes glint. Except the nervousness of the dogs, and of the soldiers standing in front of the bread ovens. No children, as if they were being kept indoors. No women, either, around the wells. No weapons leaning up against the walls, waiting to be greased. The fire in the forge is out. Eleanor looks for the stables. Behind the horses, a low door opens out onto a narrow stone bridge, and the countryside beyond. But that door is now barred by a wide wooden board. Eleanor signals her escort to reverse. At the very moment Count Thibaut appears, smiling with his arms open wide, she reins around. Stunned, her men obey. Horses neigh, and a whirlwind of dust stings the eyes. Thibaut's smile freezes. He tries to say a few words, almost starts to run. But it's too late. My mother has broken into a gallop.

Now the elm trees are heavy with night. In the forest, a circle of men raise their torches, and one of Thibaut's knights kneels before Eleanor, blindfolded. The point of a sword touches his back. He tells of the count's plans to imprison Eleanor so she would become his wife. She had guessed right. For a lord can capture a woman and marry her by force, in order to acquire her lands. Eleanor isn't surprised that one of them should seek to sequester her: she possesses Poitou and Aquitaine, after all. Hills, marshes, sea coasts, vineyards: whoever marries my mother marries this dream of a kingdom as well. Eleanor is a target. She, the huntress, knows she is the quarry. Hence her predicament and her anger.

She is ready before dawn. The knight is left knocked out, his limp body strung up to a tree.

The following night, she sends out a scout, who returns bearing bad news. Eleanor is having her hair arranged while her knights set up camp. The messenger kneels, starts to speak. Another trap will be laid at the junction of the Vienne and the Creuse rivers. Who wishes to capture Eleanor this time? The scout lowers his eyes. It is a young nobleman of sixteen years. Of which family? The Plantagenets. My mother raises her eyebrows. Granite eyes, slightly amused. This is her future husband's younger brother. This youth is planning to abduct Eleanor, marry her, and surpass his elder brother. She bursts out laughing – no, she never laughs. But the situation must appear farcical to her.

I have never met this uncle myself, nor do I care to. But there was a warning sign there. My father's line love to kill each other. They resemble those mad serpents that painters of illuminations draw inside the bellies of letters. My mother taught me restraint, discipline, and the pride of the clan. My father's clan respects nothing.

Eleanor decides to head north to ford the Vienne. She races along, skipping breaks between the stages in her journey. In the evenings, poems are sung around the campfire. Then the silk tents are pitched. Sometimes, before she retires, my mother gives a knight a sign to follow her.

One day, as the horses are drinking, my mother stands stock still. Before her, peasants are walking towards a farm. In the middle of the path, they bend down to turn over stones. Then they resume their walk and push open the farmyard gate. My mother breathes easily again. She is on her own lands. She has recognised their rituals. Here, whenever any-one approaches a house where someone is ill, they turn over stones along the way. If a living animal is underneath, the ailing person will live. Judging by the jaunty gait of the peas-ants, they must have found a caterpillar or an ant. My mother takes off her cape with the gold clasp and charges an equerry to take it to the farm. It will be a gift of renewal.

The roofs of Poitiers appear at last. The riders stop. They look at each other, their eyes filled with exhaustion, gratitude and resolve. It's the look of travellers with no memory, the look of the brave, venturing towards a city and finally reach-ing its gates. That look is one that Eleanor knows, gives, and returns. No one notices her hair falling heavily on her shoul-ders, her eyes red with fatigue, the layer of ochre dust covering her clothes.

Out on the road, a procession comes to greet her, singing the poems of her grandfather, William the Troubadour:

> *Since we see the meadows*
> *Flowering, and the orchards greening,*
> *The streams and fountains,*
> *Breezes and winds growing gay,*
> *Each of us should now taste joy . . .*

They shelter Eleanor beneath an embroidered canopy and escort her into the city.

The fervour rises. The townspeople are massed against the

walls. They are waving bouquets – lilies, lots of them, every-one knows she loves them. The streets are strewn with carpets. Musicians play her favourite airs. The songs call her "My Lord", "Fair Eyes", "Noble Lady" or "Alouette": at that moment, her face is both a conquest and a bird. They chant her name. Intoxicated by the festivities, Eleanor forgets her exhaustion. She reaches out to grasp hands, catches baskets of fruit, pats the heads of the babies held out to her. At the other end of the square, she sees her faithful lieutenants at the thresh-old of her palace. They do not hide their relief. She has returned. Freedom rises up inside her like light-headedness. She promises herself never to sacrifice it again.

She enters her palace as she would meet an old friend. Her steps recognise the little esplanade, the high oval door, then the courtyard. She walks past the chapel, the stables, and at last reaches the imposing square tower – her tower. Her ser-vants and soldiers await her, lined up in front of the two open doors. Eleanor enters and breathes in the smell of cut hay mixed with the scent of lilies. A fire is crackling in the hearth before the huge oak table. Two large wooden staircases lose themselves in the ceiling. From the kitchens comes the aroma of roasting game.

In the calm of the great hall, a messenger is waiting for her, sent by the king of France. Louis would like to know if all is well; if their years together might yet have counted for some-thing; what her plans are from now on. He does not mention

that, with the separation, Eleanor becomes duchess of Aquitaine again, and therefore his vassal. She owes obeisance and a
response to the king. Louis knows that she couldn't care less,
but above all he loves her too much to inflict this call to order
upon her. He knows that she is thinking about the Plantagenet. But he doesn't say anything about that either. It is a
magnificent letter, full of nobility and restrained pain. Today,
when men disappoint me, I unroll this message from Louis,
which I have preserved in its leather case, well hidden at the
bottom of a trunk.

At no point in this letter does Louis make any allusion to
the rumours that are torturing him. He does his best to remain
deaf to them. For they insinuate themselves everywhere, at
court and in the taverns – rumours about the relationship that
my mother is said to have had with . . . the Plantagenet's
father.

The men of the Church cry scandal. Louis has spent many
a sleepless night over them, and his courtiers seek to reassure him
with their bile: "You have lost nothing, Sire, what do you call
a queen who has slept with her future father-in-law? A whore,
a demon, a woman? A cursed creature, cast out by God. And
in any case, hasn't she been punished with her sterility? In fifteen years, she hasn't been capable of giving you an heir! She
has provoked wars and follies, loves power like other people
love parties, and listens to nothing but poems. Can you pos-
sibly love such a creature . . .?"

Of course you can. Louis and I are proof of that. The

former husband and the favourite son: what a pair we make! Each of us holding up our side of Eleanor's pedestal. We both know what is most intimate within her. Louis met her when she was only thirteen, and I have her blood running through my veins. Childhood and motherhood, those two great secrets in women's lives, we are their witnesses. That privilege makes us her ramparts.

A few days after Eleanor's triumphant return, a peasant woman presents herself to the court in Poitiers, with a package. She is shaking. She requests an urgent audience. In the royal hall, the woman kneels. She unwraps her package then bows her head and stiffens her arms as she holds out a piece of cloth to my mother. It is her silk cape. The farmer died. "He fought hard," the woman sobs, "but it wasn't enough."

On May 18, 1152, Eleanor marries the Plantagenet. She doesn't care about the rumours. She is said to be a witch, a whore, the lover of her father-in-law, so what? Her freedom shines in the world's face. It has only been two months since she separated from Louis. She didn't ask for his permission, obviously. They say he has locked himself in his palace chapel and spends his days in prayer.

In Poitiers, all the bells are pealing. My parents stand on the church steps, sparkling in the sunshine. They have just joined hands under the veil, pronounced their consent. With a swift movement, the Plantagenet holds my mother back, and takes a step forward. Now the duke of Aquitaine by marriage, he wishes to present himself alone. The townsfolk observe his squat, thick body, his orange beard. For once, my father is not wearing armour but an embroidered silk tunic with the effigy of a roaring lion with open claws, and this image seems out of place in the heavy silence. My father's eyes roam over the square. Then he bows his head, unaware that Aquitanians are never tamed by a mere greeting. Nothing moves. Eleanor, never a woman to be left behind, steps towards the crowd. A vision: her eyes look even bigger with makeup, and her mouth is as red as her dress. The gleam of her crown blends with the gold threads twisted into her hair. A deafening cheer bursts out. The people lift up their arms like an animal raising its quills. The banners unfurl: another lion, but a red one, with a twisted tail, close to a dragon — Eleanor's blazon. The men raise their glasses, the musicians their instruments. Huge puppets with grey eyes and straw hair are lifted above the sea of heads, while cascades of flowers flow down from the windows. My mother puts her hand on her heart and bows. Then she throws her bouquet of broom flowers into the crowd.

This time the country compares her to Gwynevere, the woman saved from darkness by a prince. My mother often sang this legend to me when I was a boy. She had heard it at court when she was a child herself. I came to understand the meaning of Gwynevere, the "white shadow". And I also understood why she loved the story so much: she knew that it could never happen. She knew that princesses are not saved, but spend their whole lives at the mercy of others' decisions. My mother wanted only one thing from her poets, that they should offer her an alternative. All of them praised her beauty, her courage, and ambition. She knew that the first withers, the second must be paid for, and the third, when it rots on the vine, is called wisdom. How many times, during long evenings, did I hear her encourage the troubadours by saying: "Sing to me of what does not exist"? For only literature can overcome fate, for the time of a poem.

> *Rich lady of a rich king*
> *Without evil, ire or sadness*

sing the troubadours, knowing full well that Eleanor is nothing but ire and sadness. And they celebrated her as "more than a lady" precisely because my father stopped her from being one.

But in this month of May, on the cathedral steps, she is happy – my mother, light-hearted! What do my mother's eyes look like, what does her voice sound like? At that moment, did she love my father? For the first time in her life, she is not suspicious. She puts her trust in this new husband, and in the blazing future she knows they have ahead of them – she had an inkling that it would turn out this way when they first met. He will be king, she is sure of it. And a good father too. And he will respect his promise to let her retain her suzerainty over Aquitaine.

The man who slips his arm around her waist, on these church steps, is educated, indefatigable, a strategist, an excellent fighter, and most importantly, a man of his word. Eleanor has no doubt about that. She never had a sense of him as a bully or a thief.

Essentially, because she is older than he is, Eleanor believes that she will lead the dance. This will prove her great mistake, but she is unaware of it for now. She doesn't know that this man will be her equal, and that this is the very point where their drama will be played out. My father shares the same naïvety. On these steps stand two lions, each of them sure of their ascendancy over the other. In reality, because they are too much alike, because they are equals, they will become mortal enemies.

For the time being, as she stands and faces the city, my mother smiles, with that smile that I find so hard to imagine — the one reserved for my father, who cannot, even for an instant, measure its price.

M Y MOTHER LOSES HER ILLUSIONS two years after
her remarriage.

One winter's evening in 1154, she is due to set sail from the
port of Barfleur, on the tip of the Cotentin Peninsula. In her
arms she holds her child, born a little more than a year after
the wedding. His name is William. The son Eleanor never
gave to Louis. And she is pregnant again.

The crew scan the skies. Low clouds, heavy swells, they
should delay the crossing. My father refuses. He has been
cursing the wind for weeks. No capricious sea will stop him.
His destiny calls. "England is at the end of a civil war," he
hammers, "she wants her new king." He will be the great
saviour. He must banish the looters, raze the insubordinate
lords' strongholds, recover the crown's assets, and mint new
coins. He promises power and justice, and to "prise the goods
of the poor from the rapacious hands of the powerful", as he had
announced. After which he will invade Ireland, subjugate
Wales . . . and Aquitaine. He wants a united land, under one
and the same law, more powerful than any feudal parcelling.

And when it is all over, when his shadow has covered even my mother's lands, then he will inspect his empire.

The Plantagenet strides along the quays. From a distance, his head, standing out against the dark sky, looks like a flame. Suddenly he orders the crews to embark. He cares not that night is falling, that William is small, and Eleanor seven months pregnant. His Norman barons try to dissuade him. He answers that December 6 is Saint Nicholas' day, the patron saint of seafarers and travellers.

Lightning pierces the sky in the middle of the crossing. Above, rain is sheeting down; below, the sea is demented; on all sides, the gusts' cold blades. The storm has closed its fist.

The master mariner can no longer steer the ship. He lets it drift. On the deck, my father bellows orders that no one listens to anymore. The seamen implore the sky, their eyes wet with rain. The sea plays with the ship like a ball. The waves surge up, crash down, and sweep the deck like white tongues rising from the deep. People fall, grasping for a handhold, then disappear. A mariner screams. He is dangling head downwards alongside the hull, his foot caught in a rope. Blades of water crash against his body. He waves his arms, then becomes a limp puppet, upside down, swinging in wide arcs at the end of his rope, his movement following the dance of the barrels rolling back and forth along the deck. In the grey vapour all around, nothing is visible, there is only noise. You would swear that the wind is sneering, the sky roaring with joy. The wood creaks as if it were screaming, the hull resounds with the crazed neighing of the horses. The flooded hold spits out carpenters' tools. Anyone on deck must avoid the saws and nails rushing back and forth, invisible in the swirling water. At the bow, the banners are twisting in the wind, derisory remnants of prestige. Suddenly the clouds part and reveal the fixed white eye of the moon. Everyone falls quiet and immobile in the sinister light. Then the mists close in again like a mouth, darkness falls, and the storm starts up again. The ship has two masts. The mizzenmast gives way, its torn sails beating like wings. The mainmast still holds. The canvas billows, held back to the yards like a stretching body. A few brave seamen attempt to reef it. Their shadows slowly climb up into the rigging, then a gust, then a surge of water, then nothing.

My mother has burrowed into a corner of the hold, in the stern, with her company crouched around her. She has taken William from his nurse's arms and is holding him fast against her breast. He is screaming in his wet swaddling clothes. On the floor, a black puddle sloshes back and forth. The ship regularly rises up, seems to be suspended in the void, and for a few interminable instants, all hearts stop beating until the terrible shock of slamming into the water turned to stone. Each time the ship takes flight then falls, Eleanor is terrified of dropping William. She has folded her legs up against her belly – a pitiful protection. Servant girls have been thrown against the trunks. They roll about with their arms in the air. Their blood mixes with wine from shattered barrels. My mother hears the horses' terror. She fears she will lose her children. For the first time, she detests my father.

When Eleanor at last sets foot on English soil, hands reach out to steady her. She is cold. The air is oily with a persistent mist. She slowly raises her eyes towards Dover Castle, built high on a cliff. Its walls and fourteen towers face the sea. In the middle, an enormous square keep rises up, flanked with four narrower turrets. Planted on its summit, taunting the north wind, the Plantagenet flags clack like jaws.

Two of the six ships have sunk. Men row dinghies around the harbour, prodding at the corpses of men and horses with poles.

Her hands on her belly, Eleanor can barely stand. She searches for the Plantagenet in the crowds. He hasn't waited for her. He is already galloping towards London with his Norman lords.

She sets out after him. The closed space of the royal litter numbs her. She takes William out of his clothing, rubs him with a woollen blanket. His little body is shivering. His nurse opens her bodice but he turns his head away and whines.

Eleanor breathes slowly. Her belly aches. Through the openings, she sees burned-out villages, traces of the civil war England has just endured. Trees are lying on their sides, their huge roots torn from the ground. Large pools are scattered over the landscape like medals. No sign here of the wooded slopes she knows. No animals, apart from a few dirty sheep.

The countryside is a mown heath, edged with ragged cliffs. My mother thinks of her forests in Poitou — a sudden knife thrust, a sharp pain of intense, tearing nostalgia mixed with a feeling of injustice. But this pain does not overwhelm her, it brings her certainty: she will prevail. This is elementary and colossal. No matter what occurs, she will not be daunted. And this conviction is the preamble to a boundless anger. No one can imagine that this litter, hurtling at speed through the ravaged countryside and filled with William's whining, is the antechamber of a devastating force.

On her arrival in London, she is informed that Westminster Palace is undergoing repairs. She is to install herself in the Bermondsey priory, on the right bank of the Thames. By order of the Plantagenet. It is a light-coloured building with pointed roofs edged with stone lace and angel faces sculpted in the facade smiling at visitors. Near the cloisters, a goldsmiths' workshop has been set up. Eleanor catches a glimpse of their backs bent over ivory sculptures and statues with emerald eyes. Blocks of gold in little tubs are waiting to be melted. My mother loves delicate workmanship, but today she turns away. She feels no exaltation or curiosity at the sight of the goldsmiths. She only notices one thing: the land here is damp and often flooded. William risks growing even weaker in this climate.

She is welcomed by the archdeacon Thomas Becket, and as he advances towards her, Eleanor notes the rustle of his chasuble, the gold embroidery on his stole, from which emerge a wrinkled neck, a dry chin, and a benevolent gaze – for her, the mask of cunning. She stiffens. She understands that he has been charged with keeping watch on her. A low bow, a deep voice, that's him then, the Plantagenet's right-hand man. He is unaware that in a few years' time, the Plantagenet will order his death. For now, he is in the Plantagenet's trust. My mother knows that in order to get access to the king she must go through these men. She is immediately suspicious of the Plantagenet.

She does not know where her husband is, or what his plans might be. Vague rumours reach her in the following days, of constant fighting and feasting that ends between women's thighs. When women are mentioned, one name often comes up: Rosamund Clifford. The daughter of an Anglo-Norman lord, she is said to be a great beauty. In fact, she looks like my mother – but gentler, perhaps, for Rosamund Clifford is often smiling and self-effacing. There are whispers that my father is mad about her. Whenever he can, he appears with her at his side. Is Eleanor jealous? I know she is proud. She would not lower herself to consider another woman her rival. She is the queen: the notion of putting herself on the same level as a commoner would never even cross her mind. And yet, it seems to me that this new betrayal by my father will be the impetus to the revolt. In the royal convoy, after the storm, she was certain she would not be cowed; now her sights are set even higher. In fact, the moment Eleanor understands that the Plantagenet loves Rosamund is when the possibility of war germinates in her mind. As if he had overstepped a boundary. This is how I come to understand that my mother, under her abrupt mien, is filled with high ideals. That the Plantagenet should sleep with other women is not her concern. She herself does not hold back. But love is something else. She believes profoundly in honour, loyalty, the value of giving one's word. They are worth more than life. I force myself to see her insistence as a thick wall protecting those elevated notions. Great dreamers are the toughest people I know.

The rumours blend with the racket of the work being carried out at Westminster. Thomas Becket had promised that everything would be finished in fifty days. He also informs Eleanor that she will not be able to see Aquitaine again for a long time. If she wishes to return to the Continent, she will have to stay in Normandy, the land of the Plantagenets.

At night, in her icy chamber, Eleanor cannot sleep. Motionless under her fur blankets, her hand is on her belly. She takes stock of the disaster: her husband keeps her under watch, prefers another woman to her, has removed her from power. More importantly, he will bring Aquitaine under his overlordship. He rules alone. As he sees fit. With shattering authority. This is not at all what she had planned.

She spends much of her time at her window. London is encircled by walls. A white tower rises up from below the ramparts, made of stones brought from Caen. The carpet of roofs bristles with flags: the Plantagenet's banners, all showing the same roaring gold lion. The sea air rumples and twists the cloth. Eleanor notes that the wind makes the lions bow.

She observes the only wooden bridge crossing the Thames. It's like a playhouse stage. Day and night, people cross it, arguing, buying and selling. Beneath its arches, houses rise up from the level of the river in heaving swarms – it's a miracle they don't collapse. Eleanor gazes at it and remembers a story she once heard, about knights having to cross a bridge under water. She likes that image. In Aquitaine, they say that a bridge holds the memory of the footsteps that have crossed it.

The servants prepare infusions of parsley and mint to strengthen the babe in her womb. After the Channel crossing, everyone fears that it will be born with a grimace of terror on its face. For months, my mother has been careful. She doesn't eat anything salty or bitter, she avoids the sight of a snuffed candle for fear of causing death. She deprives herself of the Oriental spices she loves so much, because they could give the baby leprosy. Yet despite these precautions, the storm might still take the baby from her.

She slowly opens a casket. Inside is a faded bouquet of lilies and a stone from the Poitou marshes in a silk bag. The village folk of her country swear that this stone protects the health of infants. Eleanor lifts up the edge of her bodice to slip the bag into the hem, next to her hidden blade.

*

One day, Thomas Becket brings her the Plantagenet's inaugural charter, which he has drawn up as the new king of England and duke of Aquitaine through my mother. In this text, he addresses his English and French subjects without any distinction. This means the people of Aquitaine will now be subjects of his empire and, like the others, be quashed and owe him fealty.

Eleanor puts down the charter, ignores Thomas Becket and goes to the window. The city looks like a marshland. Its stench rises. A dirty stream winds its way through the middle of London, the Walbrook, brimming with filth. But smells of honey, leather, and fish rise above the stink of decay, coming from the great market in Westcheap, which spreads its colours and cries from the stream to Saint Paul's cathedral. The market opens out onto a basin, and then there's the Thames, criss-crossed by Flemish and Italian boats loaded with wool and Cornish pewter. On the quays, people are disembarking, unloading, transporting, weighing. The merchants insult each other in all languages; the men are as boorish here as they are at the port of La Rochelle. The banks are full of chaos, and chaos appeases Eleanor. She forgets the Plantagenet's indifference, the dispossession of her lands, William's laboured breathing. Building sites, warehouses, jetties reaching into the Thames; and at night, fights, prostitutes, singing. Looking out over the disorder, my mother feels anger rising up.

*

One evening in February, she doubles over. People come running, a bath of mallow is heated, a cushion set up. My mother sits down. She touches the hem of her bodice which holds the marsh stone.

The delivery takes place with no mishaps. A second boy is born. Henry.

And where is my father at this moment? His secretary has the tact not to mention the name of Rosamund Clifford. But even he says he is exhausted by all his journeys. The Plantagenet is tirelessly roaming over England, Normandy, Aquitaine. He never sits still, his legs are covered in sores from kicking the horses. He listens to no one. Wherever he passes, he confiscates power from the barons, brings the recalcitrant vassals to heel, and starts the construction of new fortresses. He wants to saturate the landscape. Enclosures bristling with impenetrable defence towers rise up, the palaces of Gisors and Rouen are restored. Military engineers work day and night. My father also decides to dig wide moats to mark the boundary between Normandy and the kingdom of France, between Eleanor's new life and her old life. Louis is astounded, and comes in person to examine the long ditches along the Sarthe and the Avre. The Plantagenet cares little that these works cost a fortune. He keeps going, always wearing his hunter's coat and no gloves, except when holding his falcons. He imposes a common law and royal justice laid down in the French language. Like Eleanor, he is full of ideals, which he thinks are just, and puts into action. That's his strength, his instinct. The Plantagenet has lofty, distant, and sweeping goals, but does not see what is being hatched under his very nose. He thinks he is building his empire, but he is digging his own grave. No one goes into battle without having first evaluated the forces of their allies and enemies. He doesn't bother. Close by him, his wife cannot tolerate being betrayed. And his lords are furious. They whisper revenge. My father can't be in control of everything. One day he is in Oxford, the next in Calais, and the next in the Loire Valley, in pursuit of his brother, since all his family knows is treachery.

Eleanor follows his progress from afar. Messengers from Aquitaine bring back the news that her kingdom is not giving way to him. Already revolts have broken out. The barons of Angoulême are rebelling against the churchmen nominated and installed by the new power. In reprisal, my father throws himself on Poitou, burning and sacking villages, and celebrating his victory with a great banquet with Rosamund Clifford.

Eleanor knows she must remain patient. Anger is swelling slowly deep within her. Disillusion rises like sap. Soon a powerful determination will emerge that will lead her to carnage.

Westminster Palace is habitable at last, so my mother puts her energies into furnishing it. She wants to do away with English coarseness, to show that hers is the home of savoir-vivre and culture. Her first initiative is to bring over poets from Aquitaine. Twenty or so disembark one morning, dirty and delighted, onto the banks of the Thames, bringing a little of her country with them, having spent the whole crossing drinking and singing. There are women among them too. My mother always told me that, even if they can't rule as they might wish to, women can seize power by writing – that's why she will push her daughters towards literature and poetry.

The little group sways on the jetty. One of the poets slumps to the ground and vomits. He is dragged along by the others without any interruption in the singing, as is a second one who falls into the water and is fished out. Eleanor waits for them on the quay. Her eyes are shining. Behind her, a crowd of onlookers gathers, attracted by the noise.

The poets will have rooms, board, and money. They will write to the glory of my mother and of inaccessible women. For my mother's sake, they will put love at the centre of their poetry. Of course only someone who fears love would give it that honour. No one will explicitly name Eleanor, as a caution. This time, she will be called "Never Falters", "Star of the Sea" or "The Eagle", and everyone will recognise her behind those monikers. The troubadours are all a little in love with her. Some spend the night with her. The following day, they sing:

> *Lady, I am yours and shall be*
> *Given to your service*

And you are my first joy
And you will be my last joy
As long as I shall live

They will make up challenges to conquer one of her glances, orchards enclosed by walls of air, swords planted between two lovers. My mother will ask them to retell the Breton story of a couple named Tristan and Isolde. And then there is a tale my mother particularly loves, about a warrior called Arthur, "the king of kings". It's about a supernatural sword, a round table, and a magician, Merlin. Then another idea comes to her: to take this story of Arthur ... and to proclaim that English royalty descends from him. The poets are jubilant. They are manufacturing a legend. And my mother is placing a halo of magic around royal power.

To allay suspicion, she has the good sense to place her poets' talents at her husband's service. Who could know the determination that is rising inside her? She has the cunning to honour her artists and the Plantagenet's partisans at the same time. Songs to the glory of the royal lineage can be heard along with salacious tales.

Aquitanians need light. Tallow candles are replaced with oil lamps in the poets' chambers. They also want flavours. My mother has spices brought from India: pepper, cumin, and cinnamon will add savour to the English meats. And since English wines are undrinkable (they say you have to suck the

Kent and Suffolk brews through clenched teeth), ships unload wines from Aunis and Saintonge.

Eleanor also buys fine napery, copper basins, gold to decorate the tableware, and almond milk, which she uses to massage Henry. William has trouble breathing so she brings in incense and myrrh to cover the stench from the river. She plants a medicinal garden. She fears that misfortune will come to her two sons. Thomas Becket tells her that superstition can't protect us from anything. But every day, she sends someone to cut birthwort, which she burns under the cradle to keep childhood illnesses at bay. My mother explains the Greek meaning of its botanical name, *aristolochia*, excellent childbirth. She loves words like I love the sword.

The servants are asked to rub their teeth then swallow a paste of aloes every morning to purge their bile. Eleanor is washed in rose water, her body perfumed, her hair arranged, before she busies herself with the affairs of the kingdom. She signs payment orders, organises the palace accounts, keeps an eye on the fees due to the crown. Around her is a group of men keeping watch on her, led by Thomas Becket.

He oversees Henry's education, and shows great patience in dealing with him. The child obeys him, asks for him, sees him as a father. But in political affairs, Becket is in conflict with Eleanor. He loathes the fact that a queen is impinging on his role as Lord Chancellor. Eleanor knows this. She dictates the charters of justice curtly and in a dry tone as Becket writes, his brow furrowed, sometimes sighing noisily. She also takes care to countermand his decisions. One day an abbot complains about a lord who cut down his trees in Hereford. Thomas Becket takes the lord's side. Eleanor ignores this and decides in the abbot's favour. The legal document is delivered "by act of the king from beyond the sea", a sentence that Eleanor doesn't bother to read.

My father comes back, briefly. He gathers his barons together at Wallingford so they can swear fealty to his sons. William being of fragile health, he takes the precaution of involving Henry as well, although he is only six weeks old. Eleanor is present. She is ice cold with my father. As always, he does not see this as a sign. He moves on to something else, scolds a baron who has wrecked a peat field by galloping too fast. The assembly laugh, raise their glasses. Except Eleanor. The barons can't keep their eyes off her. I understand her well enough to know she enjoys this, but also that it is a question of principle for her. She holds her rank. In her mind, she is first and foremost the duchess of Aquitaine, and no one has ever seen a member of her lineage neglect appearances. Whenever she must show herself at the Court of Exchequer, at Christmas or Easter, she is magnificent. Her hair is decorated with flowers. Her capes are lined with gleaming fur, of a hue which is almost blue. Everyone looks only at her, and her coldness sharpens their appetites. My father cannot resist her. Everyone knows he loves Rosamund Clifford. And yet he seems to remember his queen, for after each of his departures, Eleanor finds herself pregnant again.

*

Indeed, her belly is round with a third child, when the nurse, alarmed, comes to find her one June morning in 1156. William is breathing poorly. He has not risen. My mother feels something undefinable in her inner depths, a terror shaking itself awake. She doesn't let it show, but sends someone to the garden for birthwort, which she places under the child's bed, as well as coriander, henbane root, and wormwood. A serving girl mistakenly brings back cumin seeds, known as a remedy for the eyes. When my mother throws the seeds back in the girl's face, without a word, everyone knows that the situation is serious, and the time has come to alert the king.

Thomas Becket keeps young Henry away. But at all of sixteen months, he is agitated and irritable, as if he were demanding justice.

The day progresses and soon there is nothing left of William but closed eyelids, a chest rising with every breath, translucent pallor — a three-year-old body trying to push away death. His breath whistles. In Eleanor's ears, the sound crashes like thunder.

In the kitchens, the monks are busy heating, sieving, grinding amber, preparing sachets, draughts, compresses. The serving girls go silently back and forth between the ovens and the bedchamber.

Crouched by the bed, Eleanor does not take her eyes from her boy. Her round belly embodies the irony of fate. A child is about to be born while another is dying. She draws near to his ear. The song chosen at William's birth escapes from her lips.

Eleanor has one goal, one single goal: to cover the approach of death with her voice, so that her son feels no fear. She sings, her last act of love. The hours pass and the whistling becomes hoarse. Now the little body is arching its back. My mother leans over and blows into his mouth, hoping to give him a little more air. Then, still singing his song, she lies down close to William. From time to time, she lets go of his hand to touch her stone from Poitou, sewn next to her heart.

That evening, the seam is undone. The stone will accompany her firstborn son into his grave.

On the gravestone, she has a command inscribed: "Raise up what is destroyed, preserve what is standing."

My mother enters an unknown county. The wind is icy. Nobody lives there. From behind its high walls, she hears the talk and laughter of those who have been spared. Try as she might to scrape open a passageway with her bare hands, to make and to hold more children, nothing changes. A border separates her life from others'. She walks among mothers amputated of a babe, dancing shadows humming lullabies. My mother now knows the hidden side of life.

Henry becomes the eldest.

Matilda is born a few days later.

I will arrive within a year.

I will grow up with the ghost of my lost brother, never knowing whether I am my mother's favourite only because I look like him. She will never speak of him, but I will see her, every month of June, wearing a gown with an undone seam in the bodice. And when I am consecrated duke of Aquitaine and pronounce the oath on my knees in the cathedral – "Raise up what is destroyed, preserve what is standing" – I will recognise those words. They belong to William.

L OUIS, IN TURN, HAD CHILDREN of his own, from two other marriages. But he always managed to stay in the doorway to Eleanor's life. That doorway is us. From the age of ten, our mother sends us to her first husband. This might seem rather strange, but Louis holds us in high esteem and sees us for who we are. He does not try to impose his tyr anny upon us. Most importantly, he delegates his power, so his young son, Philip, will never know the same torments as we do. He is the little brother I wish I could have had. There are eight years between us. He is a happy child, cheerful and stubborn, spoiled by his sisters, Marguerite and Alys. His father is proud of him, his sisters fuss over him – how I envy him! Philip will never have to overthrow his father. He will never cover his face with mud.

Louis is aware of this. He takes up our cause, to the point of discreetly encouraging the revolt of the Aquitanians against my father. He delights in the war that is being prepared. The two kings have always had knives at each other's throats any way. They sometimes made agreements that fooled no one and turned out to be worthless, such as giving their children to each other in marriage. Henry married Marguerite, Louis' eldest daughter, in the hope of a reconciliation between the kingdoms of France and England, and I am promised to Alys, Louis' second daughter.

This changes nothing. Louis and the Plantagenet loathe each other. And we, the Plantagenet's sons, have chosen Louis; our need for attention is that strong. One day, enraged to hear that we were at the French court, our father sent men to bring us back to England. They presented themselves at the palace in Paris, in that great Council hall my mother knows so well. They laid out their request. Henry, Geoffrey, and I were to return with all haste. Louis enquired in honeyed tones:

"Who makes this request of me?"

"The king of England," the messengers answered, nonplussed. "He asks for his sons."

"The king of England? Come now, that is impossible, since he is here, with his brothers. Henry was crowned, was he not? So what king are you talking about?"

The men took their leave with this declaration of war. His voice full of mischief, Louis asked us: "And now, would you like to see Henry's royal seal?" In his hand was a velvet cloth which he unfolded as if opening the petals of a flower. Inside was a disc with Henry's effigy, cast in heavy gold.

That day, we the princes of English birth swore fealty to the king of France. And I asked Louis to make me one of his knights.

That very evening, he organised a huge banquet for us. The women's skin glowed in the candlelight. Mercadier bawled obscenities so loud that I had to call him to order. The floor was strewn with mint. "Your mother's favourite scent," Louis whispered to me. "It was everywhere when I first met her." We smiled politely, a little surprised. My mother only loves lilies. When I mentioned this to Louis, his smile was so pained that I bit my lip.

Luckily the horn sounded. Henry, Geoffrey, and I washed our hands and took our places. We sat enthroned among the guests and the laughter, next to Louis' children. Marguerite, the eldest, tried to restrain Philip, who was jiggling to the sound of the flutes. Their sister Alys was bursting with laughter. These princesses were pretty, and I thought that Henry would be happy with Marguerite. Alys, however, seemed more timid. She was looking after Philip, settling him back onto the bench whenever he lost his balance.

I remember the vaulted hall, the slightly tasteless wine, typical of the Parisian countryside; the hands wiped on the tablecloth leaving brown stains; the damp faces of the jugglers. Mercadier could no longer tell whether he was biting into a piece of meat or a serving girl's arm. The table howled with laughter. The poultry was golden, gorged with the saffron we had brought back from the Crusades. Louis, whose stomach was constricted by the fasts imposed by the Church, hardly touched his food. But he beamed confidence and that was enough.

At the end of the meal, he demanded silence. He rose. He swore on the Gospels that he would support us against our father. Then there was a scraping of benches. The counts of Flanders, Champagne, Blois and Dreux rose in turn. They too laid their hands on the Gospels, and pronounced the same oath.

That evening, we knew we existed. We, the three banished, rejected sons, were lifted up by these voices. What did it matter that they came from a kingdom that was our enemy? Oaths were taken for us. Those promises held the taste of rebirth.

Mercadier and I celebrated this recognition in our own way. We are hewn from the same wood. Henry curled his lips as a sign of reprobation. Louis didn't see anything; he was talking with a priest. I had to gently push Philip away, he was tangled between our legs. The night was ours. The alleys of Paris smelled of mildew, a scent I still find appealing. Candles burned behind the canvases at the windows. The muddy earth absorbed our footsteps. Mercadier made a few grotesque dance moves that were ill suited to his stature, in order to avoid a cascade of vegetable peelings thrown from an upper floor. My eyes welling with laughter, I pushed him into a barbershop. The barber had already shut up shop but, on seeing my colossus, decided he would trim his beard after all. From the obscure depths of the city wafted the smells of tanneries, the lowing of beasts, the rumours of a tavern. We drank its reserves of wine dry, while a tipsy poet, standing on a table, bellowed out ditties, and a tooth-puller, fascinated by

Mercadier's jaw, tried to make him open his mouth. Mercadier paid for enough of his drink to quiet him down, then grasped him by the arms and hung him on a hook. As we left, we bawled out the poet's rhymes. Then we came into a square bustling with people. A snaking line of dancers, gushing fountains, pigs on spits, happy girls: life, at last, proud and noisy, so different from England. Without an escort or any ceremonial, nobody recognised me. Mercadier thrust his chin in the direction of a place in the square where pretty girls were being served wine. But as he turned towards it, a group of men stepped in front of him. Before I could make a move to stop him, Mercadier's enormous fist came down on two of the boors' shoulders. The battle raged. It was an exquisite fight, with fists and jugs thrown wantonly about, to the sound of the women's frightened clucking. Mercadier grabbed a bench, held it to his chest and swivelled around. After two rounds, he had a spit full of bodies bent over the bench, wiggling like hares. "Bow down before the protégé of the king of France!" he bellowed and laughed, his little eyes gleaming with joy, a reminder of the oath Louis had sworn to us, the forgotten royal children of England.

In the early hours of the morning, we staggered back through the alleyways. Mercadier pressed his hand to his temple, which had been hit by a goblet during the fight. My foot hit a spinning top, abandoned next to a laundry trough. We had to go back to Poitiers. My mother was waiting for us.

*

She was sitting before a swarm of obsequious bodies, but with a wave of her hand, we were suddenly alone with her. I told her everything, about the messengers from England, Louis' response, the banquet, and the oaths. She listened attentively. Seeing her sitting there, imperially, with her narrow shoulders under her tunic and her auburn tresses coiled about her head, with that poise that other noble women tried their best to copy, I wondered if this was how my father had first seen her. She would not have had those wrinkles at the corners of her eyes, and her face would have been less pale. But that wide forehead, those eyes like a stormy sky, and the erect hold of her head, yes of course he had seen her that way. And yet he behaved as if he were blind.

Now I try to remember exactly when everything changed, the precise instant when war against my father became inevitable to us. There is a rupture, which seems to date from time immemorial, for the troubles are as deep as winter frosts. But for us, it happened a few months ago, and I must tell that story.

For several months, my father has believed himself out of danger, convinced that he has appeased his three enemies. He has temporarily loosened the reins on Aquitaine; he has crowned Henry king – that should keep him quiet for a while, he thinks; he has obtained the Church's pardon after assassinating Thomas Becket, who had defended the rights of the Church against those of the sovereign. He was found in the cathedral, his skull open on the flagstones. It took my father three years to wash away that crime. Only Henry, who loved Becket, forgave nothing at all.

His wife, his sons, the Church: my father is sure he has lulled them all to sleep. His vigilance subsides. He devotes his time to John's future. My youngest brother is not yet seven years old. He doesn't even know how to hold a sword. But what can you expect of a child who peed into the air during his baptism ceremony? The priest pretended not to see anything. He poured baptismal water over his head while John evacuated it from below.

John returns from the abbey of Fontevraud. It's a place my mother and I love passionately — a white and tranquil place set in the countryside near Saumur. Eleanor has always looked after it. She set up an annuity to buy the nuns' garments, gifted a gold processional cross and silk liturgical ornaments, built walls around the abbey. John was out of place in that city of silence and its magnificent garden retreat.

There are long, vaulted corridors, with black and white checkerboard floors, high windows opening onto vineyards planted on terraces. The roof over the kitchens dominates everything, bristling with stone finials and covered chimneys, from which the smell of smoked fish wafts out. I remember the silence and the pallor of those stones from childhood. The air seemed to stand still. Even now, I naïvely think that Fontevraud must be capable of stopping the wind and the turmoil. John, who is all rage and capriciousness, did not belong there.

And so my father takes him back to England. He speaks to him in French, gives him puppets and astronomy treatises, shows him the workings of the Exchequer, an accounting system he holds in high regard. In a word, the Plantagenet acts like a father.

Right now, he is arranging John's marriage. The count of Maurienne would consider offering his daughter, the heiress to Piedmont. Of course, giving up one's daughter has a price, but my father is ready to pay it. With this union, he would have a foothold in Italy. His empire has yet to devour that part of the world. We, his children, have never been more than pawns at the service of his gluttonous strategies. As far as I am concerned though, my father made a mistake. When he betrothed me to Alys, Louis' daughter, he was sure that this choice would be a means to avoid war.

The audience with the count of Maurienne is set to take place in Auvergne, in February. The whole family is invited.

Geoffrey and Henry join us in Poitiers. My mother and I are back from Limoges, where we have levied taxes, laid the foundation stone of a monastery together, and inspected our fiefdoms. That progress allowed us to gauge the lords' hatred of the Plantagenet. (Some time ago, they had made a donkey bray on the ramparts and cried to the English to come save their king. In revenge, my father ravaged their domains.)

No one wants to make this journey for John. We leave for Auvergne sighing.

This is where everything falls apart. At the foot of the walls of Montferrand, the field is covered with tents and banners. The horses have been stripped of their ornaments, and are at rest, exhaling little clouds. The gonfalons gently flap in the cold air. The local shopkeepers go back and forth all day between the town and the camp, bringing poultry, fruit, canvases, thatch for the soldiers' bedding near the wagons. Deals are struck. Sometimes there are fights. Mercadier leads the squadrons into the forest to hunt wolves.

In the middle of the field, beneath a canopy of gold cloth, the count of Maurienne and my father face their courtiers. They must announce the conditions of the marriage – or, to be more accurate, how much the daughter of the count of Maurienne is worth. The two men sit in state on sculpted wooden thrones. Their swords are planted in the ground. My mother stands behind them. Her ermine cloak reaches down to her feet, and she has lowered its hood over her shoulders. A few snowflakes flit about and stick to the fur like tiny pearls. Henry, Geoffrey, and I, in leather gloves and iron helms, face our father. Here we are, in the first row, waiting for his decisions about a younger brother we do not love.

The Plantagenet starts his speech. It goes on interminably. At last he announces the price of the marriage. For John to marry Maurienne's daughter, he will pay five thousand silver marks. The count shows his agreement. It is over, we can all go home. But then, to general astonishment, my father makes another promise. He will take the kingdom of Ireland, several

English castles, and the fiefdoms of Chinon, Loudun, and Mirebeau from our inheritances, to give them to John.

A heavy silence.

This humiliation is one too many. Subjugating us is not enough for him. My father has to strip us, his three elder sons, of our lands and give them to John.

Henry pales and takes a step forward. Without thinking, I put my hand to my sword hilt. Mercadier and Geoffrey do the same. What stops me, in that instant, is my mother standing before me. Her eyes are like armour. They are brimming with a calm fury biding its time. Eleanor's rage is where our misery goes to drown. We know her. We trust her. Henry is the first to change his mind. My ribbons of shadow disappear, pushed away by grey eyes. But under our feet a chasm has opened up to the cursed winds. It is too late. We are dumbstruck, while my father, in this uproar, continues to calmly present his list of bargaining points.

Two months later, he organises a lavish gathering in Angers, his favourite town along with Le Mans. The land of his ancestors, he keeps saying, as if his lineage stopped with him. In front of a great assembly of high lords, he announces he will annex the Languedoc to his empire, since it belonged to our maternal great-grandmother. He is going about this in a perverse way, by associating us with it, Henry and me. His troops have already started to subjugate the people of Languedoc. This time, Toulouse and Narbonne thunder. The whole country knows that the Poitevins have been resisting the Plantagenet's stranglehold for years. The South follows their lead. The viscountess of Narbonne alerts the king of France, not knowing that Louis is waiting for Eleanor's reaction.

Here it comes now. She enters the hall of Poitiers and orders us to overthrow my father.

The Revolt

E LEANOR APPRAISES HER FORCES. Many of the
English lords are incensed, and will take up arms
against the Plantagenet. But one thing unsettles me. Of course
my mother has managed to bring the great barons together,
but they are asking for recompenses in return. They want
counties, domains, castles, otherwise they will not help us.
Even the king of Scotland, who hates the Plantagenet, is
demanding Northumbria, in the north of England. I sense
that my mother is going to accept. I know that I should trust
her, that her strategic intelligence has allowed her to stay in the
highest spheres of power. Even so. The cost of these alliances
is high enough to worry me.

Eleanor doesn't hear me. I watch her come and go. I notice
a striking difference: anger sustains my mother, whereas it
debases my father. His is a grotesque, eructing rage, which
brings shame to us all. It's as if he were sitting in a caul-
dron; his skin flushes red and his green eyes grow bloodshot.
The monks have tried everything. They have forbidden pepper and onions in the kitchens, prescribed lettuce sap and

infusions of ranunculus and liquorice. Nothing seems to work. My father transforms himself into a screaming elf. One day, Mercadier had to strap him up, to keep him away from a page whose cheeks he was trying to tear off. And how many times have we seen him rolling around and howling, ready to eat the straw off the floor! We are the laughing stocks of our vassals. But I must be honest: when I see him like that, I feel strange cold caresses on the back of my neck, black smoke fed by the excesses of the world, swelling with the sad spectacle of my father, soaking up each of his wails, which I hate and reject because I now recognise them as my own, because his fury is one I carry inside myself as well.

My mother's anger is of another nature. The treachery she has known has only made it greater. Once an urge, her fury became a force. It planted its fangs so deep in her memory that it became hard as stone. Her anger no longer irrigates her body, it concentrates only on the heart and its primary func⁄tion: beating in order to breathe. How I wish my anger was the same! Hers leads to acts of revenge that take the form of honour. For Eleanor, hate is anger that has aged well.

And yet, seeing her like this, a splendid fury marching and crushing, I feel a great tenderness for her. I sense an ancient pain. The poets say that when we love someone, our love touches the part of them that is most alone. I believe them, because, right now, all I can see is someone who has always been absolutely alone, who is capable of advancing without support, and resigned never to expect any. And so I should kneel down, bring her face close to mine, and ask questions, with all the gentleness a warrior can muster. Mother, what is this sorrow that gives you no peace? What do they look like, those hopes that must always remain nothing more than hopes? One cannot remake the past. But life still offers moments of rest, when a friendly presence takes off your cape and offers you a chair – moments free of expectation or menace. Why should one fear them? She would answer in her own way. Eleanor speaks a language that everyone honours but no one understands. She clenches her fists, even during banquets. But then, what is a fist? It is also a hand keeping something safe.

I give her a message from Louis. He entrusted it to me, he says, because such a good fighter cannot be captured en route. Eleanor opens it and reads it aloud. It is brief. Louis informs her that he will take part in the revolt. I try to hide a smile. So here we have it: my mother's first husband preparing to overthrow her second . . . Louis has the tact not to mention their years together. And yet, he now has his revenge, the chance to crush the man who stole his wife. Once again I admire his restraint, so foreign to my father. What words can be chosen to face such elegance? How should one answer? My mother seizes a quill. "With orders," she says. "He will muster the royal army and occupy Normandy."

Two weeks later, she wishes to dine with only Henry, Geoffrey, and me. The occasion is not relaxing – my family is never carefree. I look at my brothers. Henry roughly pushes back a lock of red hair from his eyes. He seems so old, with sadness carving bitter wrinkles on his forehead, and the brutality that is the mark of the deeply disappointed. Geoffrey stands erect, and yet everything about him breathes idleness, servility, and authority without stature. Henry only has to compliment the poultry with truffles for Geoffrey to agree with him. He will fight well, I'm sure of it, but not out of loyalty or a spirit of revenge. Geoffrey walks in Henry's footsteps, no matter what he does. He obeys him in everything. I suspect he is hoping for favours when Henry finally takes power. What would William have been like? It seems to me that, beside her lost, bitter, and obsequious sons, I am perhaps the only one who meets my mother's expectations. And I don't know if that preference is a privilege or a curse.

Eleanor sets down her goblet and speaks: "We will deploy our forces along the entire French border, from the Pyrenees to the Channel. Your father will be surrounded by an army twice the size of his own. Of course, there will be followers — cowards, courtiers, ambitious men — to take his defence, but there is no chance he will come out of this well. Geoffrey will arm his troops in Brittany; Henry will place himself facing England, since he is already her king, theoretically; Richard will tame and gather together all the lords of Aquitaine. Our allies are numerous. The king of Scotland, the counts of England, the Flemish army, my Aquitanian barons, the Bretons. And, of course, Louis."

The irony of it all makes Geoffrey gasp. No one reacts to this blunder, but Henry's eyes and mine meet. We know Eleanor. She wants the support of the king of France, whether she shared his bed or not. She is pragmatic. She raised me with the words: "Never love. Admire, devour, enrapture, but never love, or you will be fleeced." There again, I obey. It's been years since I've been betrothed to Alys. She is waiting and I will not come to her.

T HE ATTACK IS LAUNCHED IN the spring of 1173.
Henry, Geoffrey, and I, along with Louis VII, the
barons of England, Aquitaine and Brittany, rise up together
against the Plantagenet. Twenty years' worth of bitterness is
released on either side of the Channel. In England, the
despoiled barons let their fury rage. Their soldiers attack, pil-
lage, and burn the lands annexed by my father, punishing
those who are loyal to him in a tidal wave of blood and fire.
On the roadsides, the trees are thick with hanged corpses.

From her palace in Poitiers, Eleanor orchestrates the war.

In France, on June 29, these are the forces facing off. A first
army is commanded by Henry, targeting Normandy, the
Plantagenet's fiefdom. He will first attack the fortress at
Aumale, on the border between Picardie and Normandy.
The place is difficult to access. Set on a hill, it is protected to
the east by marshland and the arms of a river. A canal flows
under its wide gates. My mother has the idea of destroying the
dams so the canal waters destroy the town.

To the south, Louis' soldiers lock down Perche. They

target Verneuil, a great mass of stone and moats encircling three small burgs. At the foot of the walls, Louis plants a flag with a fleur-de-lys, a lily in honour of my mother. Carriages with iron wheels covered in mud come to a halt. Leather tarpaulins are lifted off so the siege engines can be assembled.

To the west, Geoffrey will attack the château of Dol, in Brittany.

And I occupy the south. I am at the head of the lords of Poitou and Aquitaine. They wear their coats of arms with pride, a festival of colours and shapes that my mother has taught me to decrypt. Here a chevron motif, there a bordure compony; crosses, birds, a bear; patterns of ermines, wavy vair, clover. I know them all. Among them is Geoffrey de Rançon, who has always offered refuge to my mother. He has a link with my story, like all the lords around me. I command an army of witnesses. Some of them talk about Eleanor with greedy smiles, but I don't even notice them. I am focused on the thousands of mercenaries I have engaged; I paid a fortune for that motley lot. Not a single one of them is a nobleman. They are all errant fighters, who know nothing of the art of war. Some are equipped with strange weapons, cobbled together from farm implements – I recognise a ploughshare mounted onto the end of a pole, a repurposed sickle, a fencepost. I have no confidence in these men. As soon as they get a chance, they will kill for pleasure, and I know that if we are defeated, they will immediately sell themselves to the winning camp.

*

We will march towards Le Mans, the cradle of my paternal family, skirting around the abbey of Fontevraud, which some might wish to sack. I hear the mercenaries comparing this abbey to an orgy, for it is mixed, with men and women living together. "They must have a good time at Mass," the men snicker. Mercadier tries discreetly to stop this talk. Too late. I ride up the ranks. The joker is easy to find. He is sweating. I take the time to observe him, then to unsheathe my sword. It slides slowly over his streaming temple, and with a single stroke, cuts off his ear. The mercenary screams and buckles over his horse. I rein my steed around, making sure its hooves trample the bloody organ. I take my place again at the head of the troops. Plunder Fontevraud! Do these warriors not realise my mother wishes to be buried there? It is out of the question that we should touch it.

I call for our departure. A thousand horses are set in motion behind me. That roar is a rising sap of rage and jubilation. Mercadier is exultant. A raucous song grows stronger.

> *I love it when the runners*
> *Make herds and people flee*
> *And I love the sight of men of arms*
> *Coming after them . . .*

My sword bangs against my thigh with each of my horse's hoofbeats — the iron pulse that is the rhythm of my life, beating in time with a jaunty air sung by ogres.

*

Here are the white stones of the first castle to attack. The bells peal madly. Cries are heard, the ones I know so well: "To arms!" Then the horns gather the townsfolk. The cavalcade, the creaking of hinges, the clatter of blades, the crashing of falling walls . . . War is mostly about noise. Ask any survivor who, years later, is startled by the sound of thunder. Each one tries to remember what innocent hearing was like, back when their ears were pure enough to hear only a simple storm.

I halt the march. The camp, the catapults, and assault towers are set up. It's time for the sappers. They creep up to the foot of the walls. They always start digging early, before the cauldrons of oil have had time to heat up enough to scald them. Already the first projectiles are ricocheting off their wide iron hats. But they keep at it, armed with their picks. Sappers have shoulders as hard as bronze. They will dig tirelessly and in silence, all night if they have to, until the walls slump down. Then, when the catapults suddenly rise up and their jaws let rocks fly free, I will see the walls shudder and tumble down. And as the arrows beat down on us in a black shower, I think of the stories brought back from the Crusades. Ah, the East! They say that the castle of Byblos has an elbow-shaped entrance, that the one at Seiyun has walls protected by huge earthworks to discourage sappers, and that warriors use an explosive powder whose fire is impervious to water. I will travel there one day, to acquire that knowledge of warfare. And when I return, I will fulfil my dream of building my own fortress. I have drawn so many plans for it! I will call it Château-Gaillard. It will be a stone ship built on the crest of a hill, able to cover all possible blind spots. It will have a double bailey, triangular bastions, deep, staggered defences. None of these flimsy walls that are already giving way. I had planned on sending carrion over the top of them by catapult, to infest the place. That will not be necessary. The ladders are set on the crenels. My men climb up. On the top rungs, the first bodies jerk and tumble, but behind them, the others make progress. On the ground, the gate is splintering under the blows of the ram.

This is my moment. I draw my sword.

I am seven years old. I handle a stick so well that my weapons master speaks to my mother. She says: "Give him challenges." At the quintain, I strike down all the mannequins. She says: "Give him real opponents." I topple Mercadier. I learn how to hold my lance firmly under my arm, to master the speed of the horse. I win jousts and tournaments. And then I tame the sword. Mine protests. It imposes disobedience on me. To whom? I don't know, but there is, in combat, something akin to refusal. At the final count, my great helm has taken so many blows that I can't take it off anymore. I have to lay my head on an anvil to have the dents knocked out of the iron with a hammer.

Further up the country, our armies are winning as well. After Aumale, Henry has laid waste to Neufmarché, further south.

At Verneuil, from their siege tower, Louis' soldiers have managed to throw dead rats into the water tanks. The absence of rain finished the job, and the vomiting and groaning can be heard far into the surrounding countryside. The convoys heading for Verneuil are stopped and plundered. With no resources, the town cannot last long before it falls. As for Geoffrey, he has taken the château of Dol. One after the other, the fiefdoms surrender.

On the roads, messengers pass each other at full gallop, and sometimes the peasants find one curled into a ball on the grass by a roadside, asleep. We send news to Eleanor every day.

Behind her apparent calm, she is seething at her dispossession of Aquitaine, the death of her child, the humiliation of her eldest son, the despotism and cunning of a man she thought was her ally. In a word, trust given, then betrayed. Already the troubadours are writing the tale of what they call "the loveless war".

I anticipate all those sensations I love so much. The shouts as we throw ourselves into the attack against the walls. My galloping horse gaining speed, my certainty of being at one with it. Shields clashing, a body lurching. My sword obeys, endures, carves open space. Sometimes I glimpse Mercadier's huge back, suddenly so graceful. He jumps, spins, his heavy hair flies up then falls to his shoulders again. Here he is, almost facing me. For an instant our eyes meet, and inside the iron casing surrounding his face I can see a mischievous glint, as my sword, seemingly powered by its own strength, plunges sideways into a flank, while my gaze stays fixed on his. I know all the feints. Hearing his cavernous voice bellowing my name strengthens the ardour of the troops. The landscape all around us is also at war. Red foam pours from the waterfalls. The wheat lies down in the fields that are now the last resting place of pierced bodies. I walk, my sword streaming. This is the great calm after the battle, the quiet wander through the corpses.

But as we continue to make gains, I sense that something is not right. I write to my mother: *Too much spite.* Some of the men are attacking the tuffeau stone walls with their fists. No one ever won a war without mastering their anger. And also: *Be careful, we are too dispersed.* No coalition comes out the winner of fragmentation. And, finally: *Let us not underestimate our enemy.* The Plantagenet conquered a fortress-woman and begot brave men. He is a match for us all.

July 25, under the walls of Neufchâtel-en-Bray, in Normandy, the army panics. Henry cannot hold his troops together. They are fighting blindly, with no direction.

Louis, meanwhile, is bogged down at the gates of Verneuil, where resistance is stronger than expected. The besieged townspeople have flooded the ground at the foot of the walls, to clog the siege engines. They have great reserves of arrows and food. They are not surrendering, despite the poisoned wells and the repeated attacks.

*

In August, Eleanor sends me the first message of alarm. It concerns my father. At first, he was stupefied. His wife and children in league against him! They say he stood stock still for a long while. Then he pulled himself together. He raised an army of twenty thousand mercenaries, the messenger tells me. Twenty thousand! Where did he find the money? Louis is the one who answers my question, in fevered handwriting: he has put his diamond studded coronation sword in hock. I drop the letter. A man who sells his sword has nothing left to lose. Such men are the most ferocious of all.

In five days, the Plantagenet covers the distance between Rouen and Saint-James, on the border between Normandy and Brittany. No one has ever seen a man move so fast. He demolishes all the bridges and mills in his path to isolate the population. The first Norman fortresses fall. My father plants his banner over the reconquered crenels. He sows terror among our followers. There is talk of towns being sacked in a few days, of hundreds of prisoners, of a sword so powerful it might be King Arthur's.

I grasp mine. I organise the ranks and the supplies, prepare the positions. I am expecting my father to come down towards us, but, to my great surprise, he goes straight onwards towards Paris. He throws himself on the château of Breteuil, in the Chevreuse valley. The place belongs to an English baron. Faced with my father, he abandons the castle with no protection. By the evening of August 8, Breteuil is a heap of smoking ruins.

My father sets off again, for Perche, targeting Louis now.

He sets up camp on a hillside near Verneuil. Louis looks up from the valley below and sees my father's troops in battle formation. Then he slowly looks about. The ground around him is a vast puddle of mud and blood. The banners wave idly. The fleurs-de-lys are a picture of certainty. The king of France will not have his revenge on his wife's husband.

And so he concedes. He, our ally, refuses to engage in combat. He strikes camp and retreats towards Île-de-France. I still find it hard to write those words today. Louis leaves as a coward. Atop his hill, my father relishes the spectacle. The king of England makes the king of France flee, without a fight.

The news spreads throughout the other armies. What does my mother feel at that moment? Does she understand that, for the first time in her life, she is losing? The letter she sends me only talks about us, her sons. She demands that we protect ourselves. But who is protecting her? She must now face the anger of the Church, which my father has rallied against her. The clergy are considering annulling the marriage, excommunicating the wayward wife, punishing her. They cite the Apostle Paul: "The head of the woman is the man", in the tone of indignant virgins. The archbishop of Rouen writes to her: "A woman who does not place herself under the direction of her husband is violating her natural condition. Return, O illustrious queen, to your husband and our king. Return with your sons to the husband whom you must obey."

Eleanor leans over and gently drops the letter into the fire.

*

A few days later, our father ravages Brittany. He attacks Geoffrey in the château of Dol. He swiftly takes back the place, captures seventeen knights, then decides to be done with these hotbeds of unrest once and for all. The Plantagenet is feared, he gives his savagery free rein. At the beginning of November, he tears through the Vendômois and Anjou, then heads south to Touraine and Poitou.

Here we are, then. From the ramparts of Poitiers, I see a cloud of dust thickening. Soon I can distinguish the banners with their golden lions, with open claws and jaws. Luckily Eleanor has left the city. She has taken refuge in her uncle's fiefdom, a little further to the north.

Then I understand that I will fight my father's men, but not my father himself. He is heading up to Eleanor's hiding place.

I alert my mother at once. She absolutely must leave. I arrange to meet her on the road to Chartres. From there we will go to Paris, to take refuge with Louis.

I fight like someone who once believed. I call up all the local forces – of the witches and the swirling winds. The cave walls around have been rubbed smooth by dragons' scales. I am not afraid. The Plantagenet's soldiers have bloodthirsty eyes. They are burning white hot from their victories. I know these men well. They were once mine. As I foresaw, these mercenaries rallied to my father as soon as they felt the wind change. Mercadier wants to attack them at once, but I calm him down. They lack the knowledge of war that turns a mercenary into a knight.

I establish a plan with Geoffrey de Rançon. We decide to encircle the enemy at dusk. An army of horses in a pincer movement will surprise them at the time of rest and fires. Leaning over our mounts, we stretch down and my sword skewers two men with one stroke. My wrist doesn't falter. Decapitated figures stagger on, then fall to the ground. I cry orders in Poitevin, a language these brigands don't understand. But they do know how to fight. We finish the battle hand to hand. I end up facing a helmeted man, with dried brown blood threading down his neck. I recognise him as the man whose ear I had cut off. I roar as I strike him. Behind me, Mercadier calls. Geoffrey de Rançon is wounded in the arm. He faints. I load him onto my shoulders while Mercadier protects us with blows from his axe. Sometimes I recognise a face under a helmet. A face that once fought by my side, whose tastes, laughter, and voice I know. But what use is a voice to men who have no say? My blade sinks into their shoulders just below the base of their great helms. Twice, my great-grandfather's device saves my life. Crushed by the weight of a soldier, its blade springs up at the level of his heart and the pierced body quivers, subdued at last.

At night, I lie down on the battlements, on the very stones. I raise my hand to my eyes. It is stiff, curled around an invisible hilt, I can no longer open or relax it. Behind this hardened hand lies the immensity of the sky, a bystander with empty eyes. I softly hum my birth song, but its murmur breaks. I think of Eleanor, of Matilda, of those women in the shape of stars, white and distant. An endless lament rises within me, and I don't know anymore whether it is about mothers in danger, lonesome children, or loveless wars.

I am not aware that my father has surrounded Eleanor's refuge, and that she has already secretly taken flight, disguising herself as a man dressed in trousers, a tunic, and a cloth bonnet. When the subterfuge is announced, I cannot repress a smile. When the Church finds out! A queen disguised as a peasant . . . !

She gallops at a breathless pace. She has almost left Poitou, is aiming for the Chartres road to join me. She is riding through a forest, when a net falls from a tree. My mother has the reflex of pulling her feet out of the stirrups, but while she is struggling to untangle herself, she hears the cries of her escorts behind her. She turns around just as a figure falling from a branch knocks into her, feet first. Eleanor knows how to fall. She doubles over, rolls on the ground, and grasps the dagger sewn into the lining of her tunic. Too late: the point of a blade held at her throat keeps her on the ground. The attacker frowns, hesitates, then smiles. He shouts: "We have the queen!"

And here I am, reeling on the ramparts while the mercenaries below pick up the bodies, laughing bitterly; here I am howling and striking the stone, my useless sword brandished at the heavens, insulting Mercadier whose thick arms are pulling me back from the edge. We have lost, and my mother has fallen. The torturous image of her capture will stay with me for the rest of my life.

That image is so unbearable that, to begin with, it gives me strength. I decide to continue the offensive. I am not alone. In the months following Eleanor's defeat, there are a few of us still fighting. Louis, who can't be sleeping any better than I am since his shameful retreat at Verneuil, takes up arms again to fight the Plantagenet and heads for Rouen. The pope is outraged and sends a solemn missive to Louis, who, for the first time in his life, ignores it.

For his part, Henry does not admit defeat and prepares to cross the Channel into England. Over there, the Scots are the most agitated. My father's cunning has driven them mad. They force open church doors, murder pregnant women and priests. Haggard horses roam the English countryside, mounted by corpses.

I go back to rekindle Charentes, to take back all the places laid low. But the inhabitants are too afraid of the Plantagenet's reaction. To my great surprise, La Rochelle closes its gates the moment I arrive. I fall back on Saintes, which keeps me out as well. My company and I find refuge in the château at Taillebourg, north of Saintes, with Geoffrey de Rançon.

We had spent many a long evening here in times past. I had attended sumptuous tournaments, tasted the girls. And it was in one of these rooms that Eleanor spent her wedding night with Louis, well before hatred laid down its laws. Geoffrey de Rançon was already there. He knew us as children. He was by my side during the first attacks on the Plantagenet. Of all my mother's loyal followers, he is the one I admire the most.

He greets me in the courtyard and holds me close to him with his good arm. His hair is white, his face chiselled, split by a scar on his cheek. He looks at me carefully. I see wisdom, a code of honour and the shadow of a father. With a hug, he pushes me into the hall.

The spits are turning, heavy with game. Geoffrey calls for basins of hot water for my men. He takes care to provide them with food and entertainment, settles two girls on Mercadier's lap and signals me to follow him.

The calm of the room makes my head spin. How long has it been since I've heard silence? Suddenly I remember the abbey of Fontevraud, where the nuns would eat in silence without a face in front of them. Nothing had impressed me more than this ritual. Three hundred women seated at long tables underneath the enormous roof beams, each one sitting with her back to the one behind her, in a refectory turned towards the sun ... I had understood my mother's attachment to the abbey. That tranquillity was the missing part of her.

My friend goes to stand by the fire, stokes the embers. Then asks in a soft voice, without turning around:

"And now, Richard, what will you do?"

My beard is trimmed, my hair is clean. The thickness of my cape soothes the cuts in my shoulders. For months now, I have worn nothing but my armour. There is only one thing I want to know:

"Where is she?"

He puts down the poker. His voice, oh I will remember his voice for a long time!

"First your father locked her in the tower at Chinon. Then he released her to take her to England. He is in Barfleur as we speak. Getting ready to embark. This will come as no surprise to you, but he is with your brother John, who is therefore seeing your mother as a prisoner in chains. Ah! Among the captives there is also your betrothed, Alys. With his daughter taken hostage, I am not sure how long Louis will continue to fight."

I couldn't care less about Alys and I know why. Geoffrey sits beside me. He is still looking at the fire.

"Your father will win. First, he will succeed in taking the king of Scotland prisoner. That will take some time for, apart from an Aquitanian, there is no one tougher than a Scot. Unsettled by this victory, your brother Henry will realise that it is too dangerous to invade England. He will then go to lend a hand to Louis in besieging Rouen. But your father will take him by surprise. He will set sail from Portsmouth with forty ships. I give him two days to catch his first glimpse of the roofs of Rouen, and a little more to subjugate his enemies. What do you wish to do? Face your father in combat? He might beat you. Flee to another country? Come now, you are the duke of Aquitaine. 'Raise up what is destroyed, preserve what is standing.' So this is what you will do: you will render homage to your father. It is the best way for you to protect your mother. And also, as you know, the vanquished must bow to the victors."

My brothers and I surrender within a few days of each other.

Our defeat first takes shape at Montlouis, in the countryside on the banks of the Loire that we love so much. I set foot to the ground. I hear a fluted birdsong and I recognise the coal tit. In Aquitaine we believe in invisible and chattering forces, whose signs must be translated. The coal tit is one of them. But also the vast green and brown stillness all around me. I breathe in the smell of fields, forests, streams, and suddenly this innocence fills me with grief. This beauty remains indifferent to our fate. It wishes only to grow, unconcerned about our lives. It couldn't care less about nets dropped in the heart of its forests. It knows nothing of goodness or ingratitude, and is not troubled by three defeated men and their father. My countryside will survive me with a wide smile.

That grief seems to touch us all. This time, there is no tension. War has exhausted my brothers. Seeing them dismount, I sense an unfathomable tiredness in each of their gestures.

And I find the same in my father, a discovery that astounds me. The Plantagenet never imagined that his sons would rise up against him. It has left him with a deep and painful wound, his counsellors whisper. And it's true. He stands before me, with his same squat figure, ready to pounce, but something has changed. He seems to move sluggishly. His eyelids are heavier and his lips curled in an expression of disappointment. Something has come undone inside him, in the true sense of the word, and I suddenly wonder whether, in the end, it isn't he who has lost.

Behind him appears a slim figure, willowy like my mother. She lingers in the shadows near the tents. She doesn't appear hesitant; she is just there, like a forgotten flower. This is Rosamund Clifford.

My father announces the agreement with measured words. In exchange for our submission, Henry receives two castles in Normandy; Geoffrey gets half of Brittany; I am given, in my own right, two manors in Poitou and half of the revenues of Aquitaine – a way of despoiling my mother through me.

He takes the opportunity to add that he is, irrevocably, giving John the counties of Nottingham and Marlborough, two castles in Normandy, three in Anjou, Touraine and Maine, as well as several thousand pounds in revenues.

The accord is confirmed by Louis.

We do not bat an eyelid.

Henry swallows his bitterness, once again. He still doesn't have a kingdom, and John is still creaming all the privileges. Geoffrey is already elsewhere. He has only one desire, to get away, marry Constance of Brittany, and manage his domains. I'm trying to forget my presence here, the terms I am preparing to accept, and the humiliation of a nickname that the whole country gives me. I am called "Oc e no", "Yea and

nay", the one who rises up and then surrenders. I am a dis-
grace to myself.

My gaze meets my father's. I put all my lost challenges, my
hatred and my loveless wars into it; I add my mother in chains,
the rage of not being able to rescue her, and the promise of
revenge – her legacy in the form of a closed fist.

But this is all forlorn and I know it. It is time for the ceremony of homage. It takes place in the cathedral of Le Mans,
which looks like a big white cake, swollen with vanity. I do
not care for this place. The church is full. I advance between
velvet capes lined with blades. Mercadier, whose wide shoulders dominate the crowd, encourages me with a feeble smile.
I kneel, bareheaded, before my father. In a moment I will
pronounce the oath of allegiance, and at that moment, it will
all be over. I will make my submission official. My father will
be able to order me to burn Aquitaine to the ground if he
wishes, and I will not be able to refuse. Words engage those
who pronounce them. I force myself to forget my mother
entering the tower at Salisbury. The instant that image fades,
the ceremony begins with the first ritual. I join my hands to
place them between my father's.

After the Revolt

M Y DEAR HUSBAND THOUGHT HE could destroy
me, did he? He clearly does not know me well. And
yet, he did his best . . . Five, ten, fifteen years of isolation? I've
lost count. But I have never given in to discouragement. The
Plantagenet would have enjoyed that too much. That's hatred
for you: it keeps one alive. Of course, he has wounded me
at my weakest point, by forbidding my children to communi-
cate with me. But I'm holding strong. An inch of despair
when the dim morning light seeps into my cell, an ounce of
weakness at the mention of Richard's name, and he would
gain a little ascendancy over me. That possibility horrifies me.
But so it is. You can give a man eight children and then
declare war against him.

Ever since he imprisoned me, he has been living with
Rosamund Clifford in broad daylight. He takes her everywhere. She has taken my place. She is seated next to the
Plantagenet at banquets, attends official ceremonies. During
parades, she rides under the colours of the English crown. But
then I'm not going to be the one to throw the first stone. I

didn't hold back from whatever I wanted in the way of shared nights. And then, the story of the little commoner who fell for a king ... I love it. There is something exciting about braving convention. I should know. How could I feel threatened? I am still here, and my husband knows it and fears me. With that in the balance, Rosamund doesn't carry much weight. It's an old witches precept: to bring a man down, aim to make him fear you, not to topple him. On that count, I've won. The Plantagenet sees me as a danger. After the revolt, he released the king of Scotland and formalised a truce with Louis, but for me, there was no clemency. I am the only one he has really punished. All these years, I've been waiting for the announcement of his death – my true liberation.

He has changed my prison according to his whims. Winchester, Buckingham, Ludgershall or Salisbury ... Especially Salisbury tower.

How much time have I spent in this keep? From the arrow slit that serves as my window, I look out at the trees. Their black branches wave like arms, and I see salvation there. The rain keeps falling, this English rain with its great gusts of wind, but those trees do not bend, glistening under its hard blows. I think of the trees in my country. I am filled with forests. Wherever I go, I take them with me. I carry inside me long horse rides, bristling birch hedges rising up in an eternal awakening. I pass by young fir trees whose tips have been eaten by deer, radiant copses, a grove of beeches by a pond. The lacy shadows shimmer on the ground, as the sun tries to pierce the leaves. I enter the home of oak, elm, and beech – they like growing close together, united against the light. At Fontevraud, I took long walks in the woodlands, in that scent of cold, moist earth, and I knew that around a hedge a new domain would open up, the one belonging to willow, ash, and alder, which grow far apart from each other, needing the open sky and plenty of breeze. A squeak, a rustling, that's a wild boar looking for the muddy water of a pond. In springtime, the bees cover the lime trees. Then the trees themselves seem to buzz, like great swarms planted in the earth. What other country offers such displays? And on the roads, convoys ride by, singing my name. The smell of meat wafts from the hamlets. Soon the great feasts will come . . .

But I must not let myself get distracted. Memory is a soldier with lean and tireless legs. It attacks at night. There's no point even trying to escape. It climbs your walls and crawls under your doors. It acts with no malice, but with the unhurried serenity of someone who knows their rights. It sparkles like fairy dresses, but that makes no difference. The sleeper can no longer move, and feels overcome by the cold.

That is where my defeat lies. I let myself be invaded. I lie down in my cell, and here is Richard unsheathing his sword, raising his eyes to mine; here is his handsome, anxious look. I hear the horses being brought back into the courtyard, as my sons Henry and Geoffrey return home giddy from the hunt. Their cheeks are red from racing in the forest. And now, the tranquillity of a hall and a fire, and Matilda sitting near it, always so serious. She holds Joan on her lap, my youngest, whose eyes are heavy with sleep. The voice of a poet rises, telling the story of Tristan and Isolde, their ruses to be able to love in peace. Matilda is listening. And my walls enclose all these treasures like a reliquary.

Often the gaolers mumble polite phrases as they push my food bowl towards me. They cook poultry for me and bring me messages. My support on the outside has clearly not diminished. A good sign. I am still the queen. And the darkness has its advantages. I can't see the state of my hair.

Alys insists on combing it for me. She has been imprisoned with me. She is Louis' girl, the daughter of the king of France, betrothed to Richard, and yet she behaves like the lowliest servant girl. Huddled against the wall, she jumps at my every step. If I open my mouth, she bolts up to curtsy. I observe her, a little perplexedly. Richard, promised to this shapeless, sobbing thing . . .? Fourteen years old, and the worries of an old lady! Is that why Richard refuses to marry her? Despair makes me edgy. I cannot bear spending my days with someone snivelling. I interrupted one of Alys' curtsies by lifting her chin. Her eyes were wide with adoration and terror. For a fleeting moment, I thought I saw her father's, with their heinous docility. Louis, the coward, defeated without even going into battle.

And so I took the opportunity to ask her the only question that matters: why did she not marry my son? Alys opened her mouth without a sound coming out. Streams of tears sprang from her eyes. I sighed. Was there not enough water in this country already? I firmly asked the question again. This time Alys bent double on the ground. I'd had enough, and grabbed her by the collar. I ordered her to give me a clear answer.

The Plantagenet had raped her. That was why Richard refused to marry her.

I wasn't even surprised. That's what happens when men think their desire is a right. Knowing the Plantagenet, I should have expected it. But I thought about Richard. Did he know, that his father had violated his fiancée? If he did, then who had told him? Why hadn't he talked to me about it? How much did he actually know? And then I stopped those ques-tions, because I was about to strangle Alys – she was suffocating, and you don't get an answer from a corpse.

The following nights I kept my eyes open. Not everything can be explained in this world, and I am sure that an imprisoned mother's thoughts reach her child's ears, one way or another. So Richard, I send you all my strength. Think about the fluttering eyelashes you can't see, nestled between these hills. You will stand strong. You can survive anything, including your father. He has stolen power from you, along with your future, your wife-to-be, and our kingdom. I have also learned that you are ravaging Aquitaine, on his orders. You are betraying me, but what else can you do? One respects one's oath of allegiance. I'm the one who taught you that. That's the kind of value words have. In fact, hearing is apparently an emotion. And so, my son, I'd like to tell you that I hear you.

And also that I forgive you. They tell me you act like an animal, in the evenings with girls abducted from their families, and at dawn when you are prepared to ruin your own fiefdoms. Go and massacre, since you have no other choice. I know all about suffering and humiliation hiding under your outward appearance of a tracked beast. I also know the love you bear me. And that love is something I fear as much as it makes me live. You understand me, for at heart you are just like me. Solitary, too troubled to be completely happy. We envy people with open arms, with easy words, who believe in a world with no enemies. But we must always be on the lookout. Where will danger come from, that is our abiding question. As a child you wanted to fight the storm. You needed Matilda to sing your song to settle you. And lilies, too, I wish so much that the ground of my prison cell could be covered with them. You were a force set free, nourished by my distance. If I came to you now, with a smile on my lips, ready for a tender caress, no doubt you would lose some of your superb violence. I don't rejoice in it, of itself; it merely reassures me because I can see that you can defend yourself. Will you be able to understand this? It's a mother's logic. My silences will have been your best weapons. You wanted to fight them; now thanks to them, you know how to protect yourself. And that's what matters most to me, that my son protects himself, when I know that death can come for someone only three years old.

Mother, I am plundering with the obscene joy of a condemned man. I know that you are in England somewhere, locked in a tower. I am on the rampage, and this liberty is an unbearable injustice. Can you hear me pushing back the night? Can you see the efforts I make to punish myself every day? You are my support, my only armour. One shouldn't say these things to one's mother, I imagine. But I cannot endure the fact that you are being mistreated in this way.

Richard, do you know how I get to sleep? Do you know what keeps me breathing during these terrible events? I repeat a prophecy to myself under my breath. It is skipping throughout the country from one mouth to another. Not a home where it isn't whispered, in the evening by the fire. It comes from a book that tells the story of Merlin the wizard – the Church has still not managed to replace wizards with God. People still prefer magic to religion, and that is really a sign of their excellent lucidity. This book lists Merlin's prophecies. It talks about a "female eagle with two heads". That is supposed to be me, since I have been twice queen, of France and England. And especially it says: "The king of the North holds you in a tight grip like a town under siege. Well then! Your sons will hear you. The eagle with the broken alliance will rejoice in her third fledgling." And so the walls fall away. A wave of hope submerges me, for my third fledgling is you, Richard.

I am destroying our lands. I've toppled the walls and captured our friends. All of our allies during the revolt . . . But here is the worst part: on my father's orders, again, I took Geoffrey de Rançon prisoner. Will you forgive me? I surrounded his castle where I had once taken refuge. Oh, his face like a sickle, looking at me in surprise, his hand held out to me so I could put it in chains, since the other one is injured! And I was the one who had saved him, heaved him onto my shoulders! He did not say a word. His sorrowful expression was enough. I remembered him turning towards the fire, predicting my defeat with a kindly voice. We crossed the great hall, that very same one where Mercadier and my men were carousing after the battle a few months ago. I was holding Geoffrey, this great lord, on a leash. The fact that he had been my friend for ever, that he had welcomed me after the rout, did not change a thing: my father had insisted I take him prisoner. As we left the château of Taillebourg, the men on the ramparts hollered "Oc e no" and spat on the ground.

How guilty you must feel! And if you know about Alys and your father, how cruel your loyalty to your oath must seem! Do not be afraid, and think of the prophecy. You are the third fledgling of the eagle and the summits are never too high.

I know about Alys. I have never spoken to her about it. I have done my best to flee her, as one erases a stain, a humiliation. I don't even know what has become of her. Every time the marriage is mentioned, I sidestep the question. I promise, I lie, I play for time. Do you understand now why I like the tavern girls so much? They may have known a thousand men, but my father hasn't touched them. They are pure in their own way.

We will restore everything. "Raise up what is destroyed, pre-serve what is standing." I did not overthrow your father, it's true, but I won the battle of words. There is the prophecy I spoke to you about. But there are also other texts that carry my trace. The songs, the poems, the books I commissioned or inspired are the witnesses to my victory. My army, the real one, the one that passes through centuries and surrenders to no one, is literature. The Plantagenet can bill and coo with Rosa-mund, rape Alys, lock up his wife . . . time will remember the pages I made sure were written. I have fed, housed, and encour-aged poets. I have commissioned stories that will survive me, like birds set free. They fly away out of sight, but will cross many lands. From now on, wherever I am, no matter what happens to me, there will always be books resounding with a queen locked in a glass palace, the woods of Brocéliande, and castles hidden in watery depths. No one is surprised anymore at the challenges a man must face to seduce a woman: those texts have inculcated a few rudiments of courtesy to love. I have man-ufactured dreams. And dreams, unlike lands, belong to no one. The peoples who only retain a single book will go mad. They will recite passages like donkeys chew grass. My own texts are so defiant of existing laws that they do not seek to impose their own. They are happy to be grasped by other hands, to roll in strangers' mouths, to never be read in the same way.

Over the Rhine, beyond the Alps and the Pyrenees, those places now have their own songs, their round tables, and their unfaithful wives. My grandfather, the first troubadour, would have been so proud! And in the best twist of irony, in England, the legend of King Arthur has flourished so much that the Plantagenet has decided to seek out his tomb. And to say that it was I who had the idea of associating Arthur with the royal lineage . . .

Of course, on that ground as well, the Plantagenet is trying to fight me. He has asked his chroniclers to write his version of events. I know this thanks to that gloved hand which brings me messages at the same time as my meals. I unroll the piece of paper near the slit of a window. And so this is what is being said: Henry was the only one responsible for the war. Whereas I am erased from history. I no longer exist. I read: "Henry alone was guilty. He led a whole army against his father. Thus the folly of a single man can drive a great number mad."

What a farce! As if my eldest son had an ounce of madness in him! He is incredibly reasonable – that's his predicament. No one ever turned the world upside down by being sensible. Poor Henry. I can see his face again, so similar to his father's. He was always trying to affirm himself and never really managed to do so, fettered by his father, stuck between two brothers, one a ghost and the other so flamboyant. One evening, he hosted all the knights called William. It was a game, he said, a way of passing the time. William . . . There were more than a hundred who attended, that night.

*

Today is the first day of summer. England is gloomier than ever. It knows nothing of golden fields, of cattle plodding back to the barns in the low rays of the evening sun. A country of ruins and lances, with its seasons all packed together, only capable of restraint. A prison whose moat is the sea.

I can hear the gulls. If I stand on tiptoe, I can see the cathedral. Ah, the arrogance of those who seek to rival the sky! I have a little secret joy. I like to think that, in their beautiful edifice, the men of the Church know that I am watching them. I have spent my life defying them. Thomas Becket, the bishops, or the pope: between them and me, the gospel of suspicion. When I gave back the crown of queen of France, they all but choked themselves. This time, I'm finishing them off. A wife defying her husband, with the support of her sons! A woman capable of giving orders, raising an army, organising a war, a woman who makes men her allies! For all those smooth-pated eunuchs, you might as well be talking about hell. The bishop of Rennes even wrote a pamphlet against queens: "They are as bad as servant girls, for from them flow only hatred, disputes, and plunder." He is quite right. A queen is never anything more than an ambitious servant.

The days pass, and I try to isolate a happy feeling, a talisman to help me endure the hours that follow. The first days of summer bring me a little sea air. That scent is enough to get me through a whole day. The next day, the sound of a flute, played somewhere in the city, will cheer me up for two nights. Then I am in my palace, surrounded by my poets. I am on the road, or on the tiered benches at a tournament, I am that "queen of a day in April" whose refrain, years ago, skipped through the streets of Poitiers. I tame my memory. It becomes my ally. Memory is stronger than regret, because in the end, the longing for something that has disappeared is not as strong as its memory. If I remember my castle, Richard's smile, or the game brought home from the hunt at dawn, what does it matter if I've lost them? Memory will always allow me to paint a kingdom, a joy, a hunt. There is no loss, if the memory of what is lost remains.

One day, I am informed that the Plantagenet has found a husband for little Joan. She is eleven. She will marry the king of Sicily. How far away that is! Her brothers will escort her there. Henry will cross Normandy into Aquitaine with her. Richard will take her onwards from there to Saint-Gilles-du-Gard, where Joan will embark for Italy. I don't know what her wedding gown will be like. I only know that the sumptuous escort will be led by the bishops of Winchester and Norwich. I know almost nothing, except that she is leaving without seeing me again.

These are baneful thoughts. I know. But when the cries of the crows sound so dreary and this horrible English sky is swollen with water, I give up the fight. Memory becomes an enemy once again.

I remember the day I accompanied Matilda to the port, when she travelled to her future husband. She was eleven too.

She rode like me, like a man. Behind us was a baggage train with the opulent trousseau I had prepared for the young bride. A princess of Aquitaine knows her rank. The animals were weighed down by forty trunks and as many leather bags, filled with dresses and jewels. I had added twenty-eight pounds of gold to decorate her tableware.

When everything was loaded onto the three boats, I raised my head towards the towers of Dover, which the Plantagenet says are impregnable. The fortress taunts the sea. Such absurd arrogance, compared to the drama at its feet: my daughter was leaving. She was taking her Baghdad ribbons for her festive hair arrangements, along with no small amount of confidence.

She raised her eyes towards me. Her white wrists almost gleamed. Her ship was sliding towards her husband, the duke of Saxony, twenty-seven years her senior.

Farewells are much like me, in fact. Silent, secret.

I did my best. I should have said something, embraced her, but I carry too much distrust in me to be gentle. I have advanced with the certainty that my children would live well. That was my only rule. They should live well. Was I wrong? Who are the happy few who fall asleep every night in the certainty that they are good people? I made sure my daughters slipped their cloaks on and went outside in the first light of morning, for nature makes you quiver at that time. I was told to put their bodies in corsets, to keep watch over their dreams, to fill their hours with sewing and embroidery to keep them from thinking. But my daughters know how to read, write, think, and – this is my personal touch – how to appreciate poetry. All this without a word of complaint. I have never heard them whine, or raise their voices, or even laugh, for that matter, if I'm honest. I did not know how to teach them joy, but I have armed them. My daughters will have the husbands that the game of power demands. They will have no choice, alas, but they will endure, no matter what their fate might be. Today I consider them saved, for they are out of reach. Incapable of laughter, but their heads held high and their fists clenched. Is it a mistake to seek to protect those we love?

In time, I will be able to think about my children without losing sleep. I will even learn to accept isolation and the loss of freedom. On that count, I am patient, and I believe the time will come to set the record straight. Prophecies are never wrong. However, what I cannot accept is powerlessness. It is a slow poison, an insidious venom that eats away at the mind. I hear that the news from the East is alarming; that the Muslims want to take back our cities; that the pope has called for a rescue of the Christians of Syria, Lebanon, and Palestine. I also hear about my youngest son, John, who deserves a stroke of the sword, and about the exasperated reminder Louis sent the Plantagenet that Richard should marry Alys . . . The rumours of the world flow to me as muted sounds. Their stream washes at my feet without my stepping into it. But I am stamping in frustration. I know exactly what must be attempted, what must be renounced, how to roar. And I look at trees through a slit in the wall.

Sometimes, the Plantagenet decides to grant me an outing. It only lasts a few days. There's not an ounce of mercy in that decision, only pragmatism. He needs royal authority to super-vise the kingdom if he is away too long, and he always arranges it so I can't see my children. He has placed my daughters far away from me. As for the boys, neither Richard nor Henry are ever advised of my brief liberation. John, of course, accom-panies his father, as always.

I don't know where I'm being taken. I taste the fresh air of the countryside, then I find myself in a room in a castle in Wiltshire, at Ludgershall or Buckingham. Day and night, I am under the surveillance of the king's henchmen. I have a little trick to humiliate them: I discreetly unfasten my cloak as I walk. It falls, and the soldiers have no choice but to pick it up. I ignore them. I keep walking, and they carry my cape.

When I have finished attending to the accounts, the griev-ances, the orders, and the laws, I organise an evening with my troubadours. I gather together those who are still in England, even if few remain here. They always need to be cheered up a bit. Ever since I have been a prisoner, they have had long faces. I urge them to laugh and compose. And then I close my eyes to listen to the songs of my victories. Their poems tell of freedom, of united families; they depict countries faithful like no man can ever be, bringing together the warm breath of trees and the diaphanous skins of rivers, of heaths, of dunes and marshes. My country. My troubadours offer it back to me every time.

They also bring news of other lands. The charm is broken by these jolts of the wider world. I hear that the pope is considering a new crusade to Syria. I have been there myself, on the second crusade, in 1147, when I was queen of France. We had set out from Metz for Antioch. Two years of travel. It was out of the question to let Louis go alone, and since when has the road been forbidden to queens? I speak Latin. As I well know, the word for road is *via*, and for life, *vita*. Why should one little letter have the force of a law? I had taken with me my gowns, my jewels, and all the duchesses of the realm. Never had a journey to the Holy Land included so many charming ladies. Of course, the clergy hollered that it was scandalous — a sure sign they were in rude health. The scents of the city of Antioch linger with me still, a blend of oranges, sand, and dates, with the burning sun and the polished steel of daggers.

Then I am taken back to my cell again. A far cry indeed from the East . . . I am alone now. Alys has been taken to the French court, as Louis, I'm told, is in poor health. His son Philip, fifteen years old, has started to govern. Apparently, he never stops drawing plans, inventing a new castle architecture. Let him draw! Let my former husband die! Let Alys build a life far away from Richard, since she wasn't able to defend herself! Let all those weaklings clear the floor!

With Alys gone, I have more room. I asked for the ground to be paved in my absence. A bed has been added. A bed-chamber, almost. It's already much better.

There is even some good news. A rare occurrence, but when it does arrive, sound the trumpets! I hear Rosamund Clifford is dead. Dead? Aye, answers my gaoler (he must be given a title, that one, when I get out. He reminds me of Mercadier, just as huge and just as loyal). So, dead then, and shrouded in rumour. They whisper that I poisoned her. The Plantagenet is accusing me throughout the land. He has demanded tales and songs that show my talents as an assassin. Why should I care? What makes me smile is not the fancy that I was free to do so, but rather the notion that if I had been, I would have concerned myself with Rosamund's life or death. As if I accorded her a high enough price to want to poison her! However, what made me break into a light-hearted song was the knowledge that the Plantagenet is devastated. From the confines of my tower, I even thanked Rosamund for this gift. Did he howl in fury, as he does every time fate opposes him? Did he roll on the floor, chomping on straw, his face purple with rage? Apparently, he arranged for her tomb to be covered with hundreds of candles. The only gentle consideration this man has ever shown anyone was bestowed on a corpse.

But the balance of the world demands its share of suffering. Good news comes at a price. And the one for Rosamund's death is exorbitant. Some time later, I am informed of a fearful thing: Richard and Henry are at war with each other. Now I can no longer fight. I'm suffocating. Behind the door, the gaoler's voice frantically calls my name. I let myself slide against the wall. I need to pull myself together, but my body is like William's at his death, an inert and cold mass. It is impossible to get up, or to find a way through this ashen fog that has covered everything. I hear the locks open, the door creak. Hands lift me up. I feel the softness of the bed, the fur put over my legs. I'm cold. I must certainly have given some order, for a hesitant voice rises, and recounts what happened. But maybe it is merely that I can suddenly see everything clearly myself. Maybe it is my own voice articulating what I have feared for so long, transforming catastrophes into lessons known by heart, hidden in my very depths.

Richard and Henry. Their differences were swept away in the battle they led against their father. Now that it is all over, now that they are tasting the bitterness of defeat, their rivalry has come to the surface again. And with such vigour! The Plantagenet, of course, is at the root of all this discord – always him, he only knows division. He must have sought long and hard for a way to light the fire of war between our sons, and he found it. Remembering suddenly that Henry was crowned king, he ordered Richard to give him Aquitaine. Richard refused. I can guess, I can see, how Henry clenched his teeth, finally glimpsing the chance to rule a kingdom, coming so close to his dream of governing at last. And I can also see Richard, calm and menacing, holding strong, defending the kingdom that belongs to us both. Voices are raised, come to insults, and at last the buried violence erupts. War is declared. My sons fight with the hatred only brotherhood can foster. Henry even manages to rally Geoffrey! He lays Aquitaine to waste, since he cannot obtain it – oh, the criminal strength of disappointed hopes! His brutality is terrifying; he even plun-ders the churches. My people are being exterminated. Henry is sacking my Aquitaine, and with each inhabitant he kills, it is Richard he is assassinating . With each family burned alive, it is us he is destroying. And when he chases the screaming mothers, it is me he is pursuing. I hear the bitterness of a son born after a dead brother and just before a brave one. A child, crowned but with no kingdom. A lonesome man, not a solitary one, who saw, powerlessly, how all the men around him were doomed, from Thomas Becket, the only man in whom Henry had any trust, assassinated on his father's orders, to Louis, with his cowardice. When there is so much pain, can one still call it war? asks the voice – mine or someone else's, how should I know, my limbs are frozen, and my one desire is to be with my sons. For his part, Richard is valiantly defending the places threatened by his brother. My Aquitaine is being torn apart. Angoulême closes its gates at Henry's approach, but Limoges opens its arms to him. Which doesn't stop him from stealing the town's treasure: he flees with twenty-two thousand Limou-sin sous! Limoges' fortune! My eldest son has become a brigand. This year, in May 1183, he plunders the sanctuary of Rocamadour, takes the banks of the Dordogne, conquers the town of Martel, and then collapses. He falls, the voice continues, and this fall appears almost incongruous now that spring has arrived and the lime trees are almost ready to be covered with bees. Henry grips his stomach. He spits blood and writhes, so much so that the bishop of Cahors is urgently called. His agony lasts a week. My eldest boy is departing, and I am locked here. He will slip away without knowing that somewhere in England, I am being kept on a bed soaked with tears. And as a hand sponges my forehead, Henry begs his father for reconciliation. He asks to see him one last time. The Plantagenet refuses. His oldest son is dying and he will not go to him.

However, he does give him a ring. The messenger sews the little leather bag to the inside of his coat and runs as fast as he can to give it to Henry. Run, messenger, bring this last sign from a father to a son who despaired of ever getting one. When Henry sees the jewel, he slips it onto his finger and presses the sapphire to his white lips. Then he is able to ask for a simple tunic to wear when he is laid down in church, to receive the Eucharist. That is how, stretched out on the flagstones, he finds the strength to pronounce one last request, which concerns me directly, this time: my liberation.

HER LIBERATION, YES, "THAT OUR father should liberate our mother and show clemency", those were my elder brother's last words. Blood was pouring from his mouth and soaking into the flagstones, but he pronounced them distinctly before his head rolled, and with such intensity that a messenger set off straight away to inform the Plantagenet. Henry was wearing his ring, had pressed the sapphire to his lips. At the threshold of death, he had held fast to noble values: forgiveness and clemency. After turning against me, after affronting me and devastating Aquitaine, he was at last coming back to himself.

I retain only a confused memory of the following days. I hear the bells ringing in anger, the rustle of the linen clothing Henry was wearing at his coronation and will wear in his tomb. He will be buried in Fontevraud Abbey. Faces move past, full of concern: the bishops of Cahors and Agen, the abbot of Dalon, the prior of Rozac, and others whose names I have forgotten. I meet the clear gaze of Philip, the new king of France, whom I knew as a child. I read in his eyes that we will not remain friends. Something is afoot. But now is not the time to worry about it. Now is the time for carousing, for consoling betrayed brothers. I feel Mercadier's grip as he lifts me from a table and loads me onto his shoulder, crosses the courtyard and drops me onto a bed, while the Plantagenet's sobs resound throughout the castle.

I am missing my mother. I don't even know if she has been informed. "She knows," Mercadier assures me. "Your father sent an emissary to bring her the news."

And so my father did not go himself to bring her the news of the death of their son.

Matilda arrives from Germany with her husband, the duke of Saxony. I restrain myself from running towards her. She is not smiling. She has just lost a child and is pregnant again. Just like Eleanor, years ago, when William died as she was expecting Matilda.

I press my sister's hands to my lips. A beautiful young mother in mourning, so like ours. I know so little about her. What do her days look like, what does she read, what are the landscapes she sees when she awakes? But the only thing I say to her is that she should go to England very soon. Our mother needs to see one of her children.

I have much to do. I start by stripping Geoffrey of his castles in Brittany, since he supported Henry in his war against me. I reduce this stupid little brother to nothing. He doesn't own much anymore and his lords greet him with insults. They say that he organises a tournament every day to forget his humiliation. I hope he ends up trampled by a horse.

Then I take control of Henry's men. Mercenaries, as always. I select eighty of them, men from the Basque country, as tough as they come, and have them blinded in the public square. Then I attack the citadels that had rallied to Henry, starting with Limoges. I raze to the ground the walls of that city that once celebrated us, long ago, my mother and me.

As I expected, my father asks me once again to cede Aquitaine, this time to John. And once again, I refuse.

After a few months, I can sit on a riverbank and put down my sword. The ground is soft, warm mud, which holds the shape of footsteps. It is a tranquil moment, on the banks of the Loire. One of those moments that put me back in my place. Clear or red, the water follows its course and, unlike men, couldn't care less about day or night. Eleanor's voice comes back to me. "You are my sons," she would say, "and yet you will always be less powerful than a river." I remember how, to stop the terrible flooding of the Loire, my father had built great dams all over the county of Anjou. He could not tolerate another power wilder than his own. Its majesty was spread before me, so different from gaily bouncing streams, or tame and tranquil maritime waterways. Flowing from the north, fattened with tributary waters, the Loire chiselled the earth and spread itself far and wide, crested with yellow foam and tree branches. Its banks were dangerous, ready to swallow up walkers. It could swell, overflow. Its fits of anger were fearsome. But, at that moment, it advanced before me with serenity.

And so I waited for the oaths to be lifted. Somewhere, far away, an eagle with a broken alliance would delight in her third fledgling. The time had come. It had happened, offered up by the arms of a river reciting laws under its breath. There were three of them: Henry's death would cause no sadness; my turn had come to be king of England; I would ensure my mother was respected.

She was liberated in June 1184.

She settled in Berkhamsted, in a manor to the north of London. On November 30, for her first official appearance, she chose a gown that the books are still talking about. A scarlet dress, lined with grey squirrel fur, embroidered with gold and pearls, emphasising her waist. Eleanor had grown thin in captivity.

We were gathered at the palace of Westminster. When the soldiers raised their lances, when her name resounded throughout the vaulted hall, drilling into my heart with anxious joy, when the court kneeled in a great rustle, she entered. She walked forward as she had long ago in Poitiers, her gown sliding over the flagstones. Stupefaction: she had been locked up for such a long time, and yet, she was walking among us now, blazing with magnificence. There was no need to see her to understand that. The bodies were bent towards the ground but they knew. She was a miracle, a fortress. She was my mother.

I did not bend my knees. I remained standing upright. I wanted to see. First an open collar, bordered with fur, the gleam of the pearls blending with the pallor of her skin. And then the fine neck, the catlike face, more marked now but made up with care. Something had changed. Of course, her forehead was lined with a few more wrinkles, her cheeks were less round, her figure almost fragile; but that feline grace, that firm step, and especially, those armour eyes fixing me, as I stood there among those bowing. A slight smile stretched her lips. I had sworn allegiance to my father, betrayed our allies in Aquitaine, continued to live my life while she was kept a prisoner. Yet that smile forgot it all. I answered it by bowing, with all the respect I was capable of. That was how our reunion took place. In silence and in secret.

Around me, the necks had straightened. Matilda was the last to rise up, with her round belly. But I knew her pregnancy had nothing to do with it. My sister was simply awestruck. Everyone was subjugated by the miracle. Eleanor was crushing us all, walking towards the dais where the Plantagenet was waiting for her, astounded as well. His eyes followed her, and I am sure that, at that moment, he was thinking about locking her up again. For he was rediscovering his enemy, now reborn and escorted by the memory of the revolt, by the deaths of Rosamund and Henry, by the resistance of her Aquitaine. That was where their difference lay:

my father was weighed down by his trials, Eleanor was majestic despite her trials. And yet, since their marriage, she had lost so much more than he had: the battle, freedom, two sons, the rule over her lands . . . But here she was. No doubt my father admired her too, for an instant, despite their hatred.

In any case, Eleanor ignored him. She did not look for signs of passing time on her husband's face, the russet hair streaked with white, the slightly slumped body. She advanced slowly, her eyes set on a distant point, in ghostly silence. Soon she passed me and I was able to observe that she had dyed her hair a beautiful chestnut colour, plaited it into a chignon pinned with rubies. Having arrived at the Plan-tagenet's side, she turned and looked calmly over the assembly, and it seemed to me her eyes stopped furtively on Matilda and me. Then she lightly lowered her forehead, as if this was the most natural thing in the world, so that my father could place the crown of England upon it. He did so without a word. Eleanor straightened up, her new-found power girding her forehead. Then the assembly, lost in love and stupefaction, kneeled again, as one body. Again, I remained too moved and too proud to kneel.

Louis' death had left her indifferent, I understood that very quickly. I remembered this: Eleanor forgives those who defy her and fight her, but not those who betray her. Louis' flight before my father's armies had sealed his fate. Eleanor had been his wife for fifteen years, and yet, it was over. I pleaded his cause, told her how he had been found paralysed one morning in his bed. A few days beforehand, Philip had disappeared during a hunt. The doctors thought that Louis had not been able to stand the anxiety of this disappearance, and once Philip returned to the court, the royal body had collapsed. Louis had remained bedridden, stiff, no longer able to talk nor move, and his lips needed to be wiped so he didn't drool. He died one night in September, without anyone noticing. Eleanor was listening to me distractedly. My words were all in vain. She had banished Louis since the episode at Verneuil, irrevocably. But I knew that Louis had died with his heart full to bursting with my mother. He had remarried twice but had never stopped loving her. And when Philip came into the world, Louis was the only one to secretly experience this birth as an injustice, because in his heart, he had never considered that another woman besides Eleanor would give him an heir. And so, knowing it was a lost cause, I made bold to ask her a precise question I had never dared to raise with her before.

"Mother, you gave the Plantagenet eight children. Why did you not give so many descendants to Louis?"

She plucked a ruby from her hair.

"I forgot."

My father played his best role: the great hypocrite. He gathered us all together for Christmas, at Windsor Castle. The only one missing was Matilda, who had just been delivered of a son. She had called him William.

Geoffrey had attacked me, I had humiliated him; we were reconciled again in our hatred for John, the eternal favourite, who dreamed of crushing us both once and for all. Such fine brotherly understanding! But for the space of one festive evening, we had to play our parts. Pretend to be a united family. Everyone obeyed, except Eleanor. She sat enthroned, how else to describe the poise she had acquired in prison? She had come out a less silent, a seemingly less solitary person. She smiled at the jesters, acquiesced in discussions, and allowed herself to be admired. She seemed to be among others at last, and not above them. And yet we all felt, my father in particular, that she had completely eluded us. We knew that her apparent ease was, in fact, a sign that we really should be concerned. Her advice came back to me: "Kill or let live, but never wound, for a wounded animal becomes dangerous." That was my father's mistake. A new power, infinitely more destructive, had been growing in prison. Eleanor now had the detachment of those who have seen too much to let themselves be hurt. She held the most fearsome thing that despair can sometimes produce: an indifference to death. She had become a river, a forest, a landscape – passive and slow forces, insensitive to sorrow. Betrayals, low blows, prison cells, lies were nothing against all that. And we were able to see the scope of her power when Geoffrey later died, crushed by his horse. It was during one of the tournaments he organised. He had been thrown from his saddle and the furious horse had trampled him to a pulp. My brother had died beneath the hooves of an animal, miserably, and I was the one who knelt before my mother to bring her the news. I didn't dare raise my head. What is there to see on the face of a woman who, in the space of a few years, has lost three children? Silence settled in. I was still kneeling, my head bowed. Then I felt her hands pressing my temples and gently raising my head. My mother was touching me, for the very first time. Her face was terrifyingly gentle, nurturing, and I felt my ribbons of shadow respond to that call. Our anger rose in unison. I then understood that her years of captivity had raised me up too, without my realising it, and brought me to a level where, like her, I no longer feared anyone anymore. And while Eleanor gave the appropriate orders, in a clear voice, for the evisceration of the body, its preservation in salt, and having the sendal coat made which would envelop Geoffrey, I wondered how much my own death would upset her.

My father tried once more to destroy us. He demanded that I marry Alys quickly. I was no longer afraid of him. Like Eleanor. We were suddenly alike in our great indifference towards obstacles. We were one and the same army, she and I. And when my father finally understood it, and felt the icy caress of fear, he locked my mother up again. Maybe it was fear, in fact, that made him choose the comfortable little castle of Winchester, set high above fertile country and more like a manor house than a prison, as well as more flexible conditions for her detention. The eagle must not be unduly provoked, lest she open her talons . . . This time, I knew that only my father's death would make her release possible. And Eleanor brooked no resistance. We were invincible. It was only a question of time. We needed to be patient, to live our lives, and wait for the game to be ours. The look Eleanor gave me on parting held everything that is impregnable – wide moats, forests and their murderous innocence, growing without a care for men.

"WINCHESTER? FOR HOW LONG THIS time? The very idea of sending one's wife to prison . . ."

We were at the edge of a forest. Philip's surprise appeared sincere; it echoed that of a whole country. Nobody could understand what had prompted my father to lock Eleanor up for a second time. To imprison her, after her sublime appearance at Westminster! People talked about her as though she were a divinity. Noblemen added a touch of disgust, horrified at the prospect of their own wives suddenly feeling the stab of independence. But everyone agreed on the injustice done to my mother. For the first time, the courtiers and the people were beginning to doubt the Plantagenet. He still inspired fear. But his fits of rage, which came more and more frequently, added to his discredit.

"You see that falcon?" said Philip. "I took it from its nest. I fed it lard and honey. I heated its breast by the fire. Then I cut off its claws and sewed its eyes shut. For, to be well trained, the bird must be blind. It learns to hunt then to come back to my fist by recognising my whistle. When it knows how to do all that, then its eyes are opened again."

I know all about training falcons. And I couldn't care less anyway. Philip knows I prefer to hunt wild boar. He raised his fist in its leather glove and, in one breath, the bird opened its wings and was gone.

"Neither you nor I are blind, Richard."

In the distance, under the branches, I knew that the bird was falling on its prey. Philip took a few steps forward, and I suddenly had the impression that Louis stood before me. A mad rage came over me, as it did every time I thought of him, along with supplications with no answers. I so wish I could have seen him before his death, to ask why he retreated at Verneuil. What went through his mind? Was it the fear of disappointing my mother, or of confronting my father, or the uncomfortable certainty that he was not made for combat? But I also would have thanked him. I remember the confidence he gave us, Henry's face when he gave him his royal seal cast in gold. I wish I could tell him that I often reread the letters he sent my mother, that I envied his capacity to remain so elegant, irreproachable.

"My father loved you. He often spoke of you. He said you were the son that was most similar to Eleanor . . . Ah, your mother. For her, he put lilies everywhere, including on my banner. All his life, he tried to attract just one of her glances. He never succeeded, even when they were married. Eleanor did not love him, did she? I don't blame her, you know. My father was not a very enterprising man . . . And obviously, to be with Eleanor, you need a solid character. A bit like you, perhaps. No one can get close to you. Not even your sister Matilda. Or Mercadier. People fear you, of course, but there is something else to it as well. You are always on guard, and so mistrustful that everyone gives up the effort it would take to tame you a little. I can understand your preference for easy women. They care nothing for any of those efforts, except to unfasten their dresses. But Richard, one day you will have to let yourself be touched. My almost-brother, where do we come from, you and I? In which soil did we grow up? We seem to be doing rather well, in the end. We have managed not to disappoint our parents without surrendering anything of ourselves. No? You are looking at me strangely . . . Of course, I am younger than you and I haven't yet mastered the sword. But we have passions in common. Did you know that I am also designing new fortresses? I've even started the construction of a tower in Bourges, and another one in Paris, in the Louvre. You would be impressed: they are round towers, not square anymore. Thick walls like you've never seen. Three stories. Arrow loops on many levels, so you can shoot in all directions. Ah, I'm being foolish, aren't I? Your plans for Château-Gaillard, which you can't stop talking about, probably already have all that, don't they? Anyway, I'm losing track. Listen. You've known me since I was a child. You are even betrothed to my sister Alys. That is why, in the name of the past that unites us, I owe you a certain frankness. So here we are: your father has suggested that I marry Alys to

John. And to that end, he would give him the rest of your rights. In other words, your younger brother would marry your fiancée and become king in your stead. I can see from your face that you don't like this. And you are right, although, someday or other, you'll have to explain why you are taking so long to marry my sister.

"This is what I have to offer right now. You want the English crown? I understand. And I approve, it should be yours. I've always known that. You have the broad shoulders and the prestige for it. But you will only obtain it by force. As long as your father is alive, he will keep it. So, come to the court of France. I offer you my support and my troops. First we will recover your lands, then the crown. We will bring down the Plantagenet. He has less and less support. Now is the right moment. Obviously, I expect something in return and here it is: while you are waiting to become king, you tender fealty to me. To me, not to your father. You choose France over England. What do you say? Hmmm? You are hesitating. It's a bold step, that's true. But you probably understand that you don't have many other ways out anymore. An alliance with another camp is your only salvation. Look, here's my falcon, the one with a red beak. Think about it, Richard."

Greetings to you, my dear son,

I am immediately answering your message, and thank Mercadier for bringing it. I can see that Philip has a different stature to his father; Louis was far too innocent to be king.

Philip's proposition is enticing, but risky. To kneel before France . . . England will not take it well. But since the Plantagenet wishes to reduce you to dust; since he always preferred John to you, Henry, or Geoffrey; since he locks up his adversaries instead of confronting them, then I advise you to accept this offer. Go to the French court, share Philip's table. Accept his help in reclaiming our lands then annihilate the Plantagenet. And for Philip's anger to become a weapon, tell him why you are not marrying Alys. Describe the rape scene, with details and repugnant images. And from being enraged, Philip will become blood-thirsty. His foresight has already brought you so much. Now you need to fertilise his hatred.

I know you well enough to understand that you are hesitating. Use Philip? Betray England? Sometimes I sense that behind all your victories is a sleepy child dreaming only of peace. I did try to protect you, to surround you with honour and words. But poems are not walls. Peace is an illusion, Richard — it is only two enemies slumbering. It is too late to ask ourselves questions. Henry's death makes you the heir to the throne, and some chances need to be taken by force. Your father wished to impose his shadow over our kingdom. He never wanted to pass on his power. And yet, I had been so sure of his loyalty, on those cathedral steps, that day in May 1152, when, in my wedding gown, I presented him to my people of Poitiers. That day I gave him my lands, my womb, and my future. Think about it, Richard: what does the word "peace" mean after such a betrayal? And so, yes, I call for vengeance against those who chose not to merge into the lands they were offered; against those who disfigure a common memory and transform their whims into laws; I call for war against spoiled children, against tyrants stupid enough to look at the sky as if it were a mirror.

Philip will meet the Plantagenet at Bonsmoulins in Normandy. The Plantagenet will go there with John, as usual. When he dismounts, he will have the disagreeable surprise of finding you there by the side of the king of France. Tensions will run high; you will feel it, as you have always felt danger. Tender hearts are upset by the fact that a warrior is closer to an animal than to a human. But, in fact, he uses the animal's most noble part, which is its instinct: that mute tension, invisible to the uninitiated, which grants him splendid reflexes. Of course, the proximity of men to the animal world raises them up instead of debasing them. This kind of logic escapes those who claim to know everything.

You will thus appear to be a cornered beast, hiding behind Philip when he asks your father to give back Poitou, Touraine, Maine, and Anjou. A pure formality. For I can predict what the Plantagenet will answer: "Today is not the day Richard will receive that gift." Do not take it badly. His reaction is logical. The Plantagenet would like to rule alone, but there you are. He would like to be

*the best warrior, but there you are again. And maybe he
would also like to be the only one I look at, but there you
are once more. All his ambitions are stymied by you. He
will never cede an inch of terrain. And so you will calmly
turn your back on him, and join your hands. You will
kneel before Philip. You will pay him homage out loud.
You will choose France.*

T HE MOMENT I PRONOUNCE THE oath of allegiance to France, my father steps back. He seems thunder-struck. He is pale. His mouth opens and shuts without emitting a sound. He steps back further, the barons stand aside. John looks over the scene with a cold weariness, a little strangely.

Philip seems satisfied. He does not take his eyes off the Plantagenet. He has succeeded where his father had failed: stunning the king of England. Who is now stammering in indignation, and yet without any sign of the fury for which he is known. Anger is a form of vigour, and today, the Plan-tagenet has none left.

He returns to his Normandy. Philip does not need to speak to me; I have understood. Our accord takes shape here, in the gallop of horses urged on at full speed, blades unsheathed. We set off in pursuit of my father. We have become hunters. Philip, drunk on fury, overwhelmed by shameful images of the Plantagenet and Alys, burns everything in our path. No quarter given to the country. We leave only grey smoke and corpses behind us. Not a single village escapes our wrath. The castles surrender quickly. All it takes is for Mercadier to approach the lords for them to talk. They admit they had lodged my father, thought that he was feverish, heard that he would take refuge in Le Mans. We arrive there at night. But the Plantagenet has had time to scarper, with seven hundred knights. He has taken the road to the south, no doubt towards Angers. We rein around and throw ourselves on his tracks. Now it will be easy.

Philip demands to see him at Colombiers, between Azay-le-Rideau and Tours. The Plantagenet must capitulate. He knows it. Ill, abandoned by his family and his followers, he has no other choice.

It is a scorching day. The meadow slumbers, its back gleaming in the sunshine, hardly even trampled by the men standing in a circle. The trees seem to be glued to the blue sky. I can't even hear the swallows anymore. Not a sound, not a murmur of wind. But the moment is too precious to complain about the heat. It is an exhausted Plantagenet I see in the meadow, bobbing on his horse like a rag mannequin, even paler than he was at Bonsmoulins. Years ago, I was the one bowing to him. I can remember how, after the failure of the revolt, I lowered my brow, while my mother mouldered in prison. The wheel has turned.

I scan his high round forehead, his cheeks covered in scars. His face is dripping. John, assisted by the last of the barons, helps him down. How old is he? The heat might yet carry off the old king, who asks for a drink. A goblet is held out to him. Then he wipes his mouth, turns towards me. His great helm is dirty and his hair falls to his shoulders. It used to be red. In a voice he wishes was strong, he explains that a pain has bitten at his heels, then his feet, and now it is eating away at his legs. It is time to surrender, he says, slowly blinking his heavy eyelids. He looks at me. How well I know those eyes, marsh green, so thick they look like mud! How well I know the black streaks in the middle that make them like a serpent's eyes! Time to surrender, yes, but his eyes cry revenge. That no longer matters. The ritual of truce can begin.

The first gesture of peace is to hand over the list of one's respective followers. Everyone can guess that my father no longer has many, but those are the rules. To reveal one's supporters is to engage in transparency. In solemn silence, the two kings exchange lists. Philip does not look at me. He is absolutely calm. He hands over his parchment, stamped with the royal seal. Suddenly I see this scroll as though it were a sword. But I must not move. My father grasps it and opens it with almost indecent haste. Why? Does he, like me, smell a whiff of the unthinkable? The parchment falls on the grass, and at the top of the list is John's name.

My father's knees give way. He is suffocating, grasping for the list. The knights surround him and try to lift him up. He spits out blood and incomprehensible sentences, but the troubadours will remember some of them. "My dear son slays me.

Death comes from my adored son. Shame, shame on the vanquished king." And so the news travels, far beyond Aquitaine, through England, the little kingdom of France, Flanders, the empires of the north and the east. The last Plantagenet son, the favourite, has betrayed his father. John delivered the *coup de grâce*. Everyone is wondering at what stage he met with Philip, when they sealed their agreement and, especially, why. Eleanor and I know the answer to this last question. I am the heir to the English throne and duke of Aquitaine. But John wants to be king of England. And Philip wants Aquitaine, to increase the kingdom of France. They have become allies in order to overthrow me and share out my domains. For John, it matters little that this alliance should kill his father.

The Plantagenet is lying in his chamber in the castle of Chinon. Around him are three knights who are still loyal to him. They try to make him drink, but he throws the goblet across the room. He pounds his broad chest, then, his strength spent, lets his arms fall. The nights pass. He writhes, pants, brandishes the parchment. He calls for John, asks him why he has betrayed him, cries out my name, insults us, and falls back on the bed. Then he sits up again, furious, and vituperates against Philip, then Eleanor, John, and me. Images float past of his first meeting my mother, under Louis' eyes, when he was still her husband; the lands he received and those he conquered; the long rides through the valleys of Anjou, the attacks, the feasts; the births of his children; Rosamund Clif-ford; then the revolt in his family, the first victory, the war, and John's turnaround. His memory is emptying itself. Despite all the remedies and prayers, his fever does not abate. My father breathes his last insult as others breathe their last sigh. He enters the hereafter with his body full of rage, his hand clenched around a roll of parchment.

Then something revolting happens. As the knights are arranging for his body's journey to the funeral, the servants plunder the room. The Plantagenet, king of England and Ireland, duke of Normandy and Aquitaine, count of Anjou, the most powerful monarch in Christendom, is hated enough to be stripped of his possessions. The jewels, the silver, the sheets disappear. Even the clothing is taken from his corpse, lying exposed in the castle bailey. By the time the knights return, his cape has been unfastened, his tunic and shoes removed. My father rests in the open air, almost naked.

The funeral rites take place at the abbey of Fontevraud. The troubadours will write about my impassive face. They will say I didn't grieve. And that, in fact, is the truth. My father is dead, I take his place, and I am liberated from my oath to Philip. And yet I feel nothing. But, contrary to Eleanor, I do not know if this void is caused by indifference or the great silence that comes before a rupture.

Then I throw myself on England. Even Mercadier has trouble keeping up with me. This time, I will be the one to liberate my mother. I must absolutely tell her of John's treason.

And in another way, of Philip's, who told me nothing of his scheme. I need to know what Eleanor thinks. I advance at the speed of a lost soul. I hear the first cries of "Long live the king!" as I pass, and remember the prophecy. The third fledgling of the eagle has prevailed. I see bowed heads, torches held aloft along the roadsides as night falls, sails billowing in a joyous wind. Here are the English fields, coated in fog pierced by the bright morning sun. I can only think of the barbican at Winchester, the raised portcullis, the soldiers making way for my horse. I hear singing in several voices from a small chapel next to the keep. With a shove of my shoulder, I open the heavy wooden door, which bounces against the wall. The racket interrupts the troubadours standing facing my mother. She slowly turns her head, makes a sign to the guards who appear behind me to stay still. She remains seated.

"I was just hearing a song with several voices. They blend together, it's extraordinary. You should listen. The troubadours you see here are reading these strange scores, annotated so that each of the voices finds its place. This invention comes to us from Italy."

I lower my eyes, catch my breath, gather up some calm. Then I look at her and understand. She has already heard the news. Of course. I have no idea how, but she already knows about John's betrayal and her husband's death. I calm myself and ask — because that is what she expects — for the truth behind appearances, the crucial beneath the trivial.

"What are these gentlemen singing about?"

"A shepherd who defies a dragon, and loses."

She stands up in a rustle of fabric. The words I would have so loved to pronounce with panache stay stuck in my throat. They come out in the end, hoarsely, too timidly, chopped by emotion, but at last I manage to say them.

"We have won."

And I think: we have won, but at what cost? A father killed by his sons. The *coup de grâce* delivered by his favourite. And you, Mother, locked up for so many years. Are there victories lined with regrets? Or must one always be worthy of what is a certainty? What if I am not worthy?

But, of course, I say none of this and instead I kneel before Eleanor, hoping that she will understand my exhausted relief. She lifts me up, looks out of the open door. Then she addresses the artists and the soldiers, all turned to stone by this scene.

"Bow before the king of England."

A happy time opens up for Eleanor, the first for many years. I see her come to life again. Each of her appearances is as sumptuous as the one she made at Westminster, when she came out of prison for the first time.

I delegate my power to her by general edict. I order the kingdom to obey her decisions. Her first is to liberate all the prisoners of England. She insists: all of them, no exceptions. My father, in his madness, had filled the gaols. Even poachers were mutilated. Now, the gates open, the families weep in gratitude. A few outraged reproaches are heard here and there, accusing my mother of weakness. She pays them no heed. She has suf-fered too much from imprisonment to tolerate it any longer.

Then she calls back her troubadours, assembles an itinerant court to make a royal progress to the castles, the towns and the villages, to explain that I am the king. That is incorrect. In truth, she is the queen, and always has been. And maybe this long road of treason and war was only ever leading here, to the decision I made to give her my power. Maybe I have lived knowing my only role is to offer her this regency. That's where this feeling of now being of no use might be coming from. Of having fulfilled my mission – or of having been a puppet, I cannot tell. It is a victorious autumn. The poplars rise up like yellow torches around my mother. Blazing red bouquets spring out from the undergrowth. The trees gleam with a thousand shades of fire, but this feast of colour fills me with sadness – always, the crushing tranquillity of nature, which remains untouched by our deaths. I watch the parades without really being there. People crowd around Eleanor, kiss the hem of her gown. No doubt she is reliving her moments of glory in Poi-tiers. I observe her and am happy for her, but my heart is empty, a hollow cavity beating with no energy, filled with nothing and nobody. And yet we are free and we won. So what? She smiles at me. Her eyes narrow and the colour of storms becomes the line of the horizon, so fine it can hardly be seen. Her face is different, angular but relaxed. Eleanor is relishing her freedom and the affection people show her. They stroke her horse's caparison embroidered with gold thread, and whisper songs.

Lady, rose with no thorn,
Faded bough bearing fruit,
Unploughed field giving grain,
Mother star of the sun,
No woman in the world
Can be compared to you . . .

She addresses discreet thanks to her poets, who, a few steps behind her, accompany the festivities with violins and flutes. Mercadier is on watch and pushes back the adoring crowds. Even the most remote hamlet is feasting. The people can breathe. They repeat the lines of a poem that says everything about their feelings after the Plantagenet's death:

Let me sing to you of a wonder,
The sun has set and no night followed.

The Plantagenet had ordered the monasteries to open up their stables to feed his war horses. Eleanor cancels this obligation. She founds hospitals for the poor, a monastery at Gourfaille near Fontevraud, gives the Knights Hospitaller a little port not far from La Rochelle . . . Watching her at work, I remember my father, who had built a lepers' hospital near Caen, dug out fishing reservoirs, built bridges and dykes, and what came afterwards now seems obvious to me. So many things in common could only lead to conflict. History belongs to these two giants, and I am only a pebble. So much so that, during my

coronation as king of England in Westminster Abbey, with holy oil gleaming on the palms of my hands, and the royal mantle heavy on my shoulders, I have to force myself to take the golden sceptre. I tell myself this throne is for my mother, or that it should have been for William, if he had lived. In short, I am crowned, yet feel as if I deserve nothing. My mother wears a red silk cloak, so that the whole assembly can see her and follow her movements. As she rises to start the hymns, it appears to me like a flower of blood blossoming from a wound.

I need her words so much, her advice and her acumen. But for the first time, I hate this need, even if the prospect of it being filled delights me. Oh, the stillness of an orchard in the morning — for my mother still loves that time, when she used to push my sisters outside at dawn. The orchard is an enclosed world protected by walls at the foot of the keep. It is like our bond. At this hour, the birds' chirruping is just beginning. We walk along the green and scented paths. I look at the shrubs, the first little apples in the boughs, breathe in the medicinal herbs planted among the espaliers. This is our time, free of all tension, these mornings when Eleanor tells me her strategy, as we sit on the edge of the fountain, under the trees trembling in the mauve light. Has she ever had anything else inside her but strategies? Perhaps she has; in fact, she may have had any number of regrets and dreams. The certainty that I will never have access to any of them, and that I will always remain a child behind a closed door despite our victory, is perhaps another reason why I feel so alone.

"Philip's plot with John is an early warning. Some day or other, they will conspire together to take Aquitaine from us. In the meantime, show yourself as docile. Lull Philip to sleep, promise that you will marry Alys. Do the same with your brother. Give him the title of count. Make yourself agreeable. Associate him with your glory."

I obey her — what else do I know how to do? But there is something in me that no longer follows. Something that resists and rears up, like the thrusting I feel in my sword. I meet with John. He avoids my gaze; I smile benevolently at him. I see Philip again. He stares me straight in the eyes; I don't mention his alliance with John. I promise that I will marry Alys, despite my father's violation.

I often repeat the oath of Poitiers: "Raise up what is destroyed, preserve what is standing." But every day, I feel the need to leave. I dream of voyages, of epic journeys, of the East bristling with fortresses. The situation is critical. They say that, after Jerusalem, the Muslims are threatening our cities in Syria, Lebanon, and Palestine, and that their military expert-ise is twice the worth of ours. The name of a warrior chief is mentioned: Saladin, the nephew of a Kurdish general, who is establishing his dynasty and talking of "jihad" — no one here understands the word, it clearly means a war in the name of God. Saladin is the master strategist behind the greatest exploit I know of. He took back Jerusalem in a battle whose echoes still keep me awake at night: the battle of Hittin, near the Sea of Galilee. During this offensive, Saladin prevented our twenty thousand soldiers from gaining access to the water. An enormous rocky plateau, the heat like a furnace, the lake so close but out of reach . . . Our thirsty soldiers are trapped. Saladin attacks. A child's game. Two hundred Knights Templar decapitated on the spot. God knows how much I respect the Templars, but I also must salute the enemy's skills. Which are not about to die out: apparently Saladin has a brother, Al-Adil, his equal in guile and cunning. The strength of brotherhood, which I have never known! If Henry and I had combined our talents . . . We could have set off together, a fearsome pair, rivals of those Eastern brothers. And so when I hear of the death of Matilda, in her far-off country, I don't ask any questions. I don't enquire about the cause of her death, whether she suffered, what will become of her children. I have no more context, resolutions, memories, or plans. Just a fact: my favourite sister, whom I knew so little, is dead, and my sense of dislocation appears to be permanent. It's that simple. I leave for the East, my head full of ghosts. They are my escort. Matilda walks in front of our father, then come Henry, Geoffrey, and William. And my mother's love, that king of phantoms, that chimera enthroned among the shrouds. I don't doubt it though, when she slaps my steed's hindquarters to signal the departure.

A few months earlier, when I announced my journey, my mother had not appeared surprised. She never does. The last person to surprise her was my father, and that turned out to be the death of him. We shared the roles between us. She arranged finance for the journey. She raised a tax, the "Saladin tithe", sold a part of the royal domains, cleared the accounts, retrieved one hundred silver marks that my father had left in the coffers. For my part, I assembled the lords who would accompany me. They had to be mustered and equipped, their oaths received. I gathered together sheriffs, men of justice, and treasurers. I chose trustworthy men to replace them, those who would work with Eleanor during my absence. And finally, I charged Mercadier with checking all the preparations throughout the whole country. The shipwrights built iron-barded vessels, the leather-workers made sturdy saddles, the armourers forged the toughest swords. The towns rang with the blows from the smithies. All of England prepared for the crusade.

I had enough time to reach the Pyrenees so I could punish the brigands who were looting the pilgrims on their way to Compostela, and, while I was there I met the king of Navarre and his beautiful daughter, Berengaria. The sight of her at last rekindled my desire to bite, an appetite I thought had fallen asleep. Berengaria was feasting her eyes on me. I also knew she was looking for a husband. But this was not the time for celebrating. We would see about that later. It was time to go.

The Lament of the Overthrown Father

FROM WHERE I AM NOW, *I am watching you. There you are, ready to leave for the East. You'll see, the Mediterranean is very different to the Channel. It turns out a sea can be gentle after all. I can see your crown. You are the king of England now. A fine revenge on fate . . . Nothing surprising there, if one is to believe Merlin's famous prophecy: "The eagle with two heads will rejoice in her third fledgling." For indeed I married an eagle, and my mistake was to fail to understand this. An eagle with mahogany hair and grey eyes, as voracious as I was. Both of us were at our peak of excellence, we caught each other's scent, recognised each other. Both of us underestimated the other. So similar, in fact, too close not to kill each other.*

I provoked your mother without realising it. For me, it was natural to impose myself on Aquitaine. One loves a land because one is a foreigner there. And I was. The newcomer feels gratitude towards the country that welcomes him. He will try to understand it, examine it in its furthest corners. Nobody knows a place as well as an intruder. The locals do not know their own luck. They behave like owners. They complain. Everything appears to them to be a right, not a blessing. When I set foot in Aquitaine, truly, I felt that sense of exalted gratitude. I was in a rush to tame its towns and castles. But all of them rejected me. I soon learned that the Aquitanians cannot stand to be dominated. They have independence in their blood. And yet, I had great dreams for that kingdom. I honoured it with my ambitions. I wanted it to be more powerful, with new regulations. I worked towards strengthening it, which others stupidly considered a threat. Was it a threat to wish for Aquitaine to be wrought as a unified, and thus invincible realm? I wanted to create a real empire, for nothing can be built on fragmentation. What needed to happen was for all the lands to be aligned — for England, Normandy, Limousin, Gascony, Poitou, and all of Aquitaine to have the same laws and the same coin. No one understood my plan. The Aquitanians tried to dismantle it at once. From then on, I had no scruples in extending my power. They didn't want me? I would impose myself anyway. Needless to say, your mother felt like she was being personally attacked, but I had to show my strength. I had to frighten Louis VII, who was secretly fomenting hatred against me. I was ready to build an empire, and no pale king was going to stop me. Yes, I enjoyed conquering Aquitaine, then taking Ireland, Scotland, and aiming for Italy . . . It didn't matter which land it was really, as long as I gained power. I could not be changed. Taking power means first building a road. Making the world advance as I had decided it should. I want a domain? I will have it. Not for the sake of possession in itself. But for the fulfilment of a long-held dream. Inside the man of power, there is often a child drawing the borders of a kingdom in the dust. There is also an intuition of an irremediable defeat. For while the logic of power is eternal, a man is not. He knows he is the loser. He will disappear, and his desire for conquest will be taken up by others. And so he tries to mark his time with an indelible trace, not, as one might think, out of arrogance, but as a way of attempting, in an absurd and magnificent leap, to counter that mismatch between immutable power and his own ephemeral incarnation.

I was criticised for acting alone. That's true. What can I say? I don't trust people. I can admit this to you now: the masses appear cowardly and stupid to me. Peasants, townsfolk, ministers, or soldiers — I used them all to do what they do best: follow. You will think me pretentious, and I certainly am. But I consider deciding for others as a service I render them. My action is not only more effective, it is also a good deed. For the exercise of power carries a long spellbinding tremor, a kind of intense and fleeting urge to live. One accedes to the throne not to defy death, but to celebrate life. Power is a delicate and crumbly substance, filled with subtle glimmerings. One must dominate but not crush; order but not humiliate. Create laws, coin, commerce, all as close as possible to what one considers just. Awaken and take charge of the hopes of an entire people. Not be afraid, yet know how to absorb other people's fears. Your mother and I loved those subtleties. At this stage, Richard, we are in the highest spheres of *persons of valour. Such are ambitious people — I will always forgive that noble quality. If ambition is to heave oneself up to the height of one's dreams, then I can still repeat to my sons: "Be ambitious. Even if that means overthrowing me."*

The initiative for your revolt had panache, I grant you that. Of course it came from Eleanor — everything that has great style is connected to her. Uniting her sons, the lords of Europe and her first husband against me . . . I can only bow down. Your mother, for the first time in her life, failed. But she did not lose. For today, I am the one who is no longer there, whereas she is still alive. And it was our children, and more precisely John, the youngest, my favourite, who dealt the coup de grâce. *That was my defeat. I could not survive such a shock. Even from where I am now, after all this time, I still cannot understand. I knew John was unstable and vain. But deceptive . . .? Treacherous to the point of killing me? That I didn't know.*

So now I see you, seething with determination. Longing for power. My blood roils through your veins. I hear the rustling of the ribbons of shadow that I know so well, I feel anger invading you. You are the one who resembles me the most. Henry did not have the gift of anger. Maybe I should have entrusted the throne to him, it's true, maybe I should have shared. But I didn't trust him. He would have dilapidated our fortune, lost our territories. He would have followed.

But you . . . You are different. You love hunting wild boar. You are the only one, of all the aristocracy, to appreciate that beast. Because the boar is a solitary animal, but also fierce and brave. Its head is never raised to the sky, but always kept at ground level. It is just like you.

And still, I died without any love from my children. Naked, alone, lost. Weakened by the revolt hatched by my wife and led by my sons, then struck down by John, the one I cherished. I must have been the worst husband and father to have sowed such hatred . . . But even so! Did I not conceive eight children with Eleanor? Can that be called a disaster? She will always be the most beautiful woman I ever knew. When she appeared at the palace at Westminster, after her liberation, her splendour frightened even me. No wonder I locked her up. She had become too dangerous. I don't trust anyone clever enough to break rank. But that apparition astounded me, I'll admit. I took the measure of my wife, as an adversary. That kind of discovery always comes with a touch of admiration. To discover the power of one's enemy is a noble surprise. But an enemy is an enemy, even if she is your wife. And yet . . . This is not the time for lying, Richard, I can tell you now: how many nights I spent, ignoring Rosamund's peaceful breathing, thinking about how we met! How many nights I raged that I had to neutralise that greatness! What a terrible irony: I was married to my equal and therefore could not live with her. That day in the palace of the Île de la Cité, in Paris, when I saw her for the first time, was constantly on my mind. She was the queen of France, sitting at Louis' side. I had come to meet the king, to pay him homage. I recited the oath, my eyes fixed on Eleanor. Even you, Richard, with your fickle heart, have never been able to rid yourself of her. Her grey eyes seep into anyone she looks at, turning them to stone. But I was the wind, I was conquest. I did not want to be turned to stone.

That was where Rosamund was able to bring light into my life. My errant and glorious life as a fighter, with my legs lacerated by the long gallops — she took care of it. Eleanor kept her fists clenched; Rosamund laid her hands on my shoulders. She had the same build as your mother, perhaps a little frailer. I love women with fine bone structures, who look ready to crack, but who, in fact, are harder than bronze. Of course on that count no one could rival Eleanor, with her exceptionally fine wrists, her slim ankles, Eleanor, with her angular face like a cat's. Everything is a delicate miniature, everything is solid and unsettling. I like women with deceiving looks. But your mother went too far, she reached my level. Rosamund, on the other hand, did not aspire to reign. She was good-natured. With her, I could allow myself a misstep. She was an Eleanor who had laid down her weapons. She could be enchanted by a rhyme, smile frankly, or cry. The world was not a threat to her. She was at peace, whereas Eleanor was always on the lookout for danger.

Your mother, Richard, always pretended she couldn't care less about Rosamund. I never believed her. Betray Eleanor! No one would dare! But I did. I am not in the habit of receiving orders. I had done my duty, making heirs. Four sons! I had fulfilled my mission. And mixed the useful with the agreeable, for on that count Eleanor deserves her rank of woman among women. But these are not things a son should hear. For the same reason, you *will hear nothing from me on Alys, your betrothed. Yes, I strayed, yes, I failed to restrain myself, yes, it's shameful for her and for you. That is all I will say. You won't find me doing penance, I can't abide regrets. And anyway, be honest: Alys, fit for you? Come now. Fragile and weepy, raised in silk and sadness — you would be bored to death. To say nothing of her feminine ways, close to nought. You who love expert and supple tavern girls with no ties in life besides those on their tunics, you can thank me. I saved you from a sinister marriage.*

You see, Richard, now that I am no longer here, somehow I can look at what I've been through without flinching. Except my children's hatred of me. I haven't managed to accept that. That they should defy me is in the natural order of things; that they should league together with their mother, so be it — I am well placed to know Eleanor's charisma; that they should start a revolt against me, that's even admirable; but that they should hate me, that is too hard. Richard, you detest me. But isn't hating someone the best way to forget how much you love them? I am probably too optimistic. What have I done, but be myself? I am a battler, a daredevil, a king. Was I supposed to transform myself at the birth of my sons? I hung on to power, chose another woman who didn't want me dead. All that came naturally to me and was therefore, I imagine, unpardonable. But just wait until you become a father, Richard, and you will see how difficult it is. You will see that there is no challenge more brutal. To be a father is to pass on a treasure — made of time, values, and pride — and one day see that treasure thrown to the ground and trampled by those to whom it was given. To be a father is to understand nothing. It is to try again to gather up those magnificent things from the very depths of oneself, which were given in a gesture of absolute generosity, and at the very instant when one tries to repair them, the child's hand again grasps and breaks them, this time into a thousand pieces. To be a father is to cry in front of an empty treasure chest. It is to have delved into one's childhood for what one thought was the very best, and to have it thrown in one's face. It is to hear the laughter of one's children turned to demons. Such an abomination bleeds into the world and taints it for ever: since such a reversal is possible, then a father can no longer read a book, for it might burn, or see the sky fill with light, for who knows whether it might not be torn asunder over one's head? To be a father is to lose one's innocence.

The Departure

WE ARE WALKING IN THE orchards of Chinon, at dawn. Eleanor's voice rises, piercingly pure like the light of these early hours. I hear the war chief she has always been:

"Richard, this is the situation. Three kingdoms have united to take back our Christian lands in the East. France with Philip Augustus, the Germanic empire with Frederick Barbarossa, England with you. Barbarossa's army already set off months ago. It's the largest of the three, two hundred thousand men. I regularly receive news. It is bad. The expedition has turned into a disaster. The Germans have always underestimated chaos. They have great dreams and are highly organised, but they forget that disorder always takes revenge on those who despise it. Do you need proof of this? No sooner had they crossed the Danube than they were attacked by Serbian and Bulgarian bandits. Regular ambushes, with the added pleasure of poisoned arrows ... And the bandits' favourite pastime is to hang their enemies from trees, head down. Fine tinsel, don't you think? Barbarossa's soldiers kept going as best they could. They passed into Turkey, braving more trouble from the Turkish soldiers. Imagine this: the emperor Barbarossa is seventy years old, trying to maintain his troops. They are scattered and starving. But they keep advancing, and almost reach the Syrian border. On June 10, there they are on a plain. It is split by a flooding river coming from the moun-tains, as if an enormous beast had clawed the ground all the way down from the summits. I have always repeated this to you: you are my son, and yet you will always be less powerful than a river. Barbarossa dismounts. He is thirsty. He feels weak. He enters the water. He is surprised by the current. Its cold hands strike the backs of his knees. He falls. It pushes down on his neck, drags him to the bottom. Struggling is no use. The weight of his armour finishes the job. It is over."

I am dumbstruck. The Germanic emperor is dead?

"Drowned before his army's eyes. They had to retrieve his body. The soldiers covered it with vinegar, but it rotted any-way. His remains were buried in haste, in Antioch Cathedral. I was there during the first crusade, with Louis. Antioch . . . Four hundred square towers on a wall the likes of which you have never seen, following the line of the rocks and the moun-tains. Over there, you'll find orange trees, a river called the Orontes, and a very dry wind. Everything is ochre. The men are magnificent. It was one of the rare beautiful moments of my life."

I don't dare ask her what the others were.

"It will soon be your turn to go, and Philip's as well. His

reign is somewhat lacking in heroism. And of course, he has just lost his wife, who succumbed while giving birth to dead twins. Like any weakened monarch, Philip will seek victories. Beware of him. You grew up together, when Louis was still alive, but that didn't stop him from betraying you by allying himself with John. And never forget this: you are his exact opposite. Contrary to what is generally thought, differences bring people together, but when they are too pronounced, they can also bring war."

Too many similarities can also start wars. That's what happened with her and my father. So when can two people love each other?

"As for you," she continues, "your deeds are excessive. You are the best warrior, you've had one girl after another, your wars are memorable. You are too sanguine and you let no one near you. Philip loathes excess. He avoids extravagance, bends to the rules, and prefers to renounce an oath rather than face a confrontation. He loves breaking his word and hates all books, except the Bible, which he can recite with his eyes shut. He sees you as a mighty threat. Not only because he knows you are more valorous than him, but also because, since you are the incarnation of his exact opposite, Louis preferred you to him."

This avowal pierces my heart. At this very moment, I have to bow my head to pass under the branch of an oak tree, and I feel as though I am bowing to the memory of Louis.

"You will leave together from Vézelay, but make sure your

troops quickly separate from the French. You'll be safer that way. The further England is away from France, the better it is for her. You will advance in the midst of a small group of trustworthy men, always the same ones, whom Mercadier will lead. The Templars will escort you as well. Everything is ready. You must now take back two cities that belonged to us, which Saladin will defend tooth and nail: Saint-John of Acre and Jerusalem."

My last task before departure was to read out the rules of discipline during the crusade. This is when the breath I had been trying to hold in, hoping that distance would give it the space it needed to live, burst forth. It must have grown impatient somehow, with the imminence of our departure. Before my subjects, my voice was more cutting than I would have wished. I read through the list of penalties: "Any man who kills another man aboard ship will be tied to the corpse and thrown overboard. If he kills him on land, he will be buried alive with him. A thief will have his head shaved and boiling pitch poured over it." Eleanor observes me, with some surprise. And while a fearful murmur ripples through the assembled troops, she smiles gently.

That breath of anger follows me from Vézelay to Jerusalem. It takes possession of me, preceded by the ribbons of shadow that war and sadness had lulled to sleep. Now they are liberated with a majesty I can no longer deny. At Lyon, the bridge collapses under the weight of the two armies. The corpses are so numerous that they cover the surface of the Rhône. My own cries follow me into my sleep. Later on, Mercadier tells me that he had the impression of seeing the Plantagenet.

Philip and I meet up in Messina, in Sicily. I put my army into ships at Marseille. Then, with Mercadier, the Templars and a small squadron, I take the road for Genoa, Pisa, Ostia, Salerno. Mercadier observes me. He cannot see the ghosts all around us, those misty uncomplaining figures, each one carrying a sliver of my memory. William's pale little body, with his smoky face, leads the march, his hand in Matilda's. My lost souls do not protest when my fury rises. That same foul breath that pushes me to steal falcons from Italian peasants, to attack a Greek convent and dislodge the monks, to tumble saleswomen, and finally, to push my men to sack the outskirts of Messina. When the inhabitants mass together under my windows to insult me, I hear myself give the order for the port to be burned, the notables' residences seized and the gallows filled. I calm down when the king of Sicily offers twenty thousand ounces of gold for me to leave. Philip demands his share, I can hardly repress a smile. It's obviously out of the question.

I obey my anger, fed by my mother's letters which I unseal alone, in the evening, in the scent of the orange trees.

One evening, Philip opens the red pavilion flap with an abrupt gesture, knocks over a stool, and stands before me, trembling with indignation. I remain seated, busy pulling apart a piece of game cooked with saffron. Philip does not shout, for he is, indeed, incapable of excess. In a hard voice, he criticises my violence, my egotism, then he gets to his real grudge, the humiliation held in a single name: Alys, and my promise, still not kept, to marry her.

I think of all the gold collected in the coffers. Of the fortresses in Syria that I will soon discover. But at the mention of Alys' name, I cannot contain myself. I can no longer bear being coerced. And I've had enough of traitors hiding as reasonable men. I prefer frankness, even if it is brutal, for savagery, whether in word or in deed, has the merit of always being sincere. And so I wipe my mouth and stand up. I slowly advance towards Philip, who doesn't step back but imperceptibly gathers all his composure. I stand very close to him. I could topple him with a thrust of my shoulder. In almost a whisper, I announce that I will not marry his sister, that it is impossible to be with a woman my father has had his way with, even under duress, that certain stains cannot be washed away. I add that I prefer whores to dirty princesses. I ignore his face beading with sweat and I inform him of a letter I received from my mother that very morning: she is on her way to Sicily, accompanied by Berengaria of Navarre. This is the woman I shall marry.

Philip weighs anchor a short time later. He heads for Saint John of Acre. That same day, my mother disembarks at Messina. She is bringing me Berengaria. It has never been said in so many words between us, but it is high time I produce an heir, otherwise all the power will rest with John.

Protected by the best knights, escorted by her eternal troubadours, keeping an eye on my future wife, Eleanor has crossed the Pyrenees, travelled through Provence then Italy. She disembarks in Naples, where Mercadier is waiting for her. Now she stands before me, in the warm night of this Mediterranean spring. We are occupying the king's residence. He will return to it once we have left. In the meantime, we are making the most of this palace, which resembles a basilica, all cupolas and porches. Here they know nothing of walls. The stones open out into bay windows onto gardens. The court lives outside. The banquet is even held on a terrace, under a round roof, facing the sea. The air smells of salt and thyme. Light curtains waft between two ancient columns. We are holding ourselves awkwardly, unsettled in our habits, for at home we dine before fires in lofty castles. From the corner of my eye I can see Mercadier cooing into the ear of a servant girl with a coppery complexion as she leans over him to serve him wine.

Eleanor doesn't even look tired. She is dressed in a gown of pink samite, scattered with feathers. With a wave of her hand, she refuses to have her wine diluted with water. The taster takes a sip, and when he confirms that it is not poisoned, the festivities commence. The meal begins with local fruit: figs, peaches, lemons. The parade of dishes is a fireworks display, saffron for yellow, cinnamon for brown, alkanet for red. The fish have pearls where their eyes once were. The poultry's feet are covered in gold, their gleam plays with the rubies sewn onto the gowns. I had asked for lilies to be brought to cover the floor, but in Sicily there are none to be had. For dessert, my mother takes several helpings of sugared almonds, thick compotes, and candied rose petals. She even enjoys the bitter taste of bigarade oranges, while Berengaria, who is used to sweeter Spanish flavours, recoils from them.

My fiancée is simpering, waiting for a sign from me, but mothers have the favour of the first look, that's how it is. When Eleanor's grey eyes cross mine, I feel a terrible nostalgia overwhelm me, a sense of solitude from before my departure, and maybe from an even earlier time. The relief of seeing her arrive in Messina and the joy of being with her again have disappeared. All that remains is the mad wish for a safe haven. The sadness of being without it, of having to wander, as if in search of a lost treasure, fills me with anger. Maybe in every man's life there is this brief instant when he looks at his mother and feels alone. I am certain that this sadness will disappear the moment she sets foot on her ship.

The servants start clearing the tables. We rise to retire to our private apartments where spices steeped in honey are waiting for us. Eleanor dips her fingers in, seems to enjoy them, and I wonder what kind of a child she was. She is talking with a courtier now about visiting sugar-cane plantations the following day – the Mediterranean islands apparently have them – she also wants to visit the spice merchants, to take back whole cases of spices to France ... A queen, always curious, never sated, a tactician with a hard mind, braver than all the men around her, and the incarnation of a great mystery, that is how she appears to me, whereas Berengaria is overwhelmed by the heat, sweltering by my side, and only able to express herself with supplicating smiles. I know I will have to wait until dawn, in an orchard, to talk to Eleanor. I yield at last, and turn to Berengaria.

"How was the girl?"

"She's from Navarre."

"She'll get over it. Breathe in the scent of these lemon trees . . . It's so acid it stings your nose! There is nothing in Aquitaine that smells like this. Speaking of Aquitaine, your brother John is piling one perfidy upon another to take it back. Just as I predicted. Oh, come now, don't stiffen up like that. Concentrate on your voyage. You will soon discover the East."

"Very well, Mother. The East."

"What does that bring to mind, for you, the East?"

"The battle of Hittin. Do you know what happened?"

"Tell me."

"Our soldiers set up camp on the rocky hillside. They had no access to the lake, which was blocked by the enemy. They spent the night with no water, without even a drop for the horses. Meanwhile Saladin was giving his troops hundreds of skins of water. He waited for the sun to be at its zenith before he set fire to the scrub around our soldiers. The bitter black smoke, the heat, the panic . . . The attack was easy. Twenty thousand men executed."

"And our cities were taken from us. You forgot to mention that part. Tiberias, Caesarea, Jaffa, Nazareth, Ascalon . . . Saint John of Acre. Jerusalem. The battle of Hittin sealed Saladin's conquests. What do you find in battles, Richard? Which is the one you never dare wage, and that you constantly replay in every fight?"

"They say that, when he took Jerusalem, Saladin let the Christians go free."

"And turned the churches into stables."

"Mother, those Muslims are great warriors. You can't take that away from them. They are also doctors, mathematicians. And writers, and we so love books."

Then a whirlwind rises. Something too big for me, which I was wrong to defy, for this is the first time that I have contested anything. Some storms look like slate eyes, whose calm is so deep that no pity could reach it. Eleanor looks at me for a brief moment, and behind her authority, her poise, and the outrage I have just committed, I also sense a fear. A new dread, of the possibility I could die, or of what is awaiting us, after so many challenges. That veil disappears at once. The morning seems peaceful again. My mother takes up her walk in the orchard, as if nothing has happened.

"You will disembark at Saint John of Acre. Our allies have been besieging it for two years. The fortress is very solid. It is protected by a powerful garrison, has plentiful provisions, and Saladin is keeping us at bay. Reinforcements have arrived from Italy, Denmark, Hungary, England, and France, to say nothing of the Templars. With no result. Saladin pushes us back and Acre resists. Our soldiers have nothing left to eat. They are grazing on roots and devouring their horses. Your arrival is eagerly anticipated."

T HE FIRST THING I SEE is the castle of Marqab, on
the Syrian coast. My ship sails beneath its ramparts.
Inside is a garrison of a thousand men and five years of food
supplies. The fortress rises high on a rocky outcrop. I'm glid‑
ing over the water past my dream. I don't ask to dock, I stay
on deck. Sometimes dreams are meant only to be glimpsed.
Later I learn that Marqab belongs to the Hospitallers, that
Saladin wasn't able to take it. All the castles I see will remind
me of this one, a splendour of rising stone, stretching its mas‑
sive neck to the sky. What does the lucky sky see, when it
looks down on these fortresses? A face. An enormous mouth,
made of a double circle of walls, towers as dark as eyes, bot‑
tomless pits linked together by stone passages so fine they
look like long eyelashes. My engineers explain that these
Christian bastions owe everything to the Muslims. We cop‑
ied their ploys. I think of Antioch with its ramparts and four
hundred towers; of Damascus, never conquered, where
Louis had to retreat after only four days of siege. Every night,
in the light of the torches, I draw my Château‑Gaillard, as I

will have it built one day. It will be made of dreams glimpsed from a ship.

June 8, 1191, after an interminable crossing, my twenty-five ships, loaded with hundreds of knights and their mounts, along with projectiles, wine, food for eight months, and an abundance of fodder, come into view of the coast of Saint John of Acre. Thousands of haggard men stand up, hesitantly at first. Then my name rolls from one mouth to the next, and finally bursts out over this miserable camp. It's also taken up by Philip's men, who did not receive the same welcome. The trumpets sound. Fires are lit, the crowd becomes unruly. The Templars stand in ranks on either side of the jetty. We take our first steps on dry land. Mercadier, hoisted up on others' shoulders, is already shaking a wine barrel. I remain immobile. Standing on the dock, I take stock of my sublime, impregnable enemy.

And so, here you are, fortress. You really are the proof that stone grows like grass around here. Let me get to know you. Your flanks are covered in a glacis. My sappers will not be able to dig under you to topple you. Behind your enormous gate, I guess that the entrance is elbow-shaped. Impossible, therefore, to charge you with a ram. And maybe the angle of your slopes has been calculated so that a horse cannot gain speed galloping up them. That seems likely.

To the south, you are protected by the sea. In the north and the west, your walls meet at a right angle, where you have built a bastion called the Cursed Tower. You have integrated a huge rock, facing the east, into your ramparts, supporting another fortification, the Tower of Flies. You have two gates. The first opens onto the port, the second onto a harbour exposed to the fearsome westerly wind. You have skilfully managed to exploit wind, sea, and stone to defend yourself.

Your walls are several layers thick. You have allowed for very high arrow slits so your soldiers can aim for the ground. You do not have a keep, that's not part of your culture. But you do have a defence system built on several levels, so that no one can come near you.

Behind the ramparts, I imagine there are several baileys, underground water tanks, pipes, and food reserves. And ten thousand men ready to hack us to pieces, hardly weakened by two years of siege.

In summary, you have organised yourself so that no one can pierce your walls. You know how to protect yourself. You punish those who approach you from the front. You have hid/ing places, secret stratagems, and your endurance is your strength. Very well. I know that kind of temperament. It is my mother's.

The men stand still. My voice covers the din. It is the same voice that listed the penalties before departure, one threatening enough for the laughing soldiers to turn into puppets baking in the sunshine. I want my engineers to set to work, immedi/ately. The catapults must be assembled, the ladders, assault towers, and polished rocks I brought from Messina unloaded. All the Knights Templar on the coast will be called in as reinforcements. I want local geometricians and carpenters. They must be showered with gold so they will deliver their secrets to us. All enemy ships near by must be attacked and the prisoners identified, to bring me their men of science. Those who refuse to collaborate will be killed.

And so this very evening, a hundred or more bearded men stand before me. Mercadier is keeping an eye on them. These men will become my own. I need their knowledge, which I will carry back to France. They know how to dig, or polish, or set up barricades. Most of them are rope-makers, ironmongers or blacksmiths, but some practise medicine, mathematics, or the military arts. One of them spends the night explaining to me how to make scimitars. By morning, I know how to produce the strongest of steels. I put fire and huge vats at this man's disposal. He will teach my troops how to blend, temper, and forge an alloy of iron and charcoal. Another man, named Hakim, is a doctor. He speaks very softly. I ask him to go through the camp to look after my ailing soldiers. From far off, I see him leaning over the dying, supporting their heads, using strangely soft gestures I don't recognise, taking out vials and potions, while all around him cries resound, along with the clanging of hammers and the creaking of ropes pulling up the palisades. In the workshops, the smell of leather is so strong one would think it was urine. Under a tent, men are tracing plans and giving birth to prodigious machines. Their calculations are all about balance, displacement, counterweights.

The machines take shape. They have names, like the bells in my country. The great catapult is called the Bad Neighbour, the assault ladder with the grappling hooks the Cat, and I feel like I'm leading a carnival when I launch the attack. The catapults reach back and spit out their rocks. They are so flexible and easily manoeuvrable that the men can recharge them day and night for months, if need be. The ladders are set against the slope of the fortress, covered in leather and animal skins, the only way to keep them from igniting under the Greek fire that the warriors throw down from their walls. The assault towers advance relentlessly, and if one topples, another one rises up behind it at once. For the moment, each breach made in the walls, each little advance is pushed back by Saladin's troops, who have reinforcements from an Egyptian company and the lord of Mosul. But my men are holding strong and shooting unstintingly. Already Saladin has lost control of the sea. He can no longer get supplies into the city. And because water is scarce, the inhabitants are reluctant to flood the ground to bog down our towers.

One night, Saladin decides to directly attack our siege engines. He penetrates the camp. The alarm is sounded. I leap up, go to find Philip and Mercadier, but we barely have time to rush at his troops before they retreat, beaten off by our first lines of soldiers.

I send a message to Saladin asking for a meeting. He refuses.

From now on the catapults alternate throwing stones and

carrion. The putrefied corpses of cows and horses fly through the air; sometimes a limb falls off, but the main thing is that they land behind the walls so they will spread an epidemic. Then I ask the geometricians to study the emplacement of wells so we can poison them. Philip tries to step in, to suggest a few ideas, direct my men. He needn't bother. My beautiful fortress will fall. It will take two more months of repeated daily assaults, of stones smashing at the walls, for it to show its first signs of weakness. My raids in Sicily and Cyprus have provided enough wealth for us to want for nothing, men, munitions, victuals. And we have time on our side. Saladin knows it. Yet he wishes to continue the fight. This is not the advice he is given by the governor of Saint John of Acre, who begs Saladin to surrender.

On July 12, I receive a message from the besieged population. They are surrendering, against Saladin's wishes. He is horrified to see my banners suddenly planted on the ramparts. As a man of honour, he bows to the decision of the local people. He evacuates his camp to the road to Sephory, some distance away. I allow him to do so, and organise our meeting. We will negotiate my victory.

Our armies are now face to face. Between us stands the disembowelled wall of Saint John of Acre, its stones flowing out like innards. The whispering wind is bloated with sand. Saladin and I step forward from the ranks. Our steeds approach each other slowly. Behind me, my army is alert.

Mercadier is in the first row, ready to intervene. Philip, with a sullen look, is boiling with rage. He would have liked to be in my place. But I am the one who made the city fall, and it is me whom the enemy wishes to meet.

Saladin advances towards me. Slender chest, blue tunic, turbaned head. Our mounts reach each other and stop. We will both speak in turn, facing the opposing army. I can only see his profile. He is not looking at my men, but far off into the distance. Bony face, thin eyebrows, olive skin, carved jaws, brown beard. So, here he is. I speak first. My voice is not as hard as I would have wished:

"Acre shall be delivered to me with everything she contains, her ships and her military reserves. I demand two hundred thousand pieces of gold, the liberation of one thousand five hundred Christian prisoners and the restitution of the Cross. Then I will spare the besieged."

He hardly seems to hear me, his eyes lost in the distance. In the great silence, he whispers as if we were alone:

"And so you are Richard the Lionheart. Even my people tell stories of your great exploits. A great warrior, a great horseman. You come from a fierce lineage, I believe. I have heard about your mother."

"I have Saint John of Acre."

"She is not docile, is she? She doesn't deliver herself to the first one to come along. It takes time, and a certain intelligence, to approach her."

"Saladin, with all the respect I owe you, you have lost."

"Not completely, not yet."

He turns and stares at me. Then I understand he is ill. His eyes, bordered with black lines, are filled with a net of thin red veins. Under his turban, I wager he doesn't have a single hair left on his head, just as he must have lost his fingernails — he is wearing gloves. I know this ailment, which has decimated my troops. I also understand that the watchful figure behind him is his brother. Saladin follows my gaze. Then he addresses a short nod to me and reins about.

That very evening, I send him Hakim.

GREETINGS TO YOU, MY SON. I have received your letter. It seems you have converted to the oriental dream . . . But beware of chimeras. This jihad, which they are claiming, and which intrigues you so much, has aims that are much more political than religious. Saladin may be pious, but it seems obvious that this holy war greatly favours his own personal ambitions. Faith allows him to legitimise his attacks, the taking of cities, and thus to consolidate his supremacy. The man is erudite, courageous, constant, filled with incontestable faith. But the man of religion is never far from his double, the man of power.

Mother, what if it were simpler than that? What if one could believe in a union between Christians and Muslims? The people here cite a Muslim high functionary who visited our lands here in the East. He observed that the local populations have been able to keep their assets, that the taxes levied are minimal. He even says, I'm citing this from memory: "The Muslims praise the conduct of the Franks who are their enemies."

The man you cite is called Ibn Jubayr. He did, in fact, travel
through our Christian states on returning from a pilgrimage to
Mecca. He also calls Christians "pigs". On a message we found
when I was in the East, we are called "dogs". And your dear
Saladin wrote to the Emir of Yemen: "We must use all our
power against the cursed Franks."

And wasn't the Koran translated here, to explain how infer-
ior it is to the Bible? Mother, let me cite the Abbot of Cluny:
"Whether we give the Mohammedan error the shameful
name of heresy, or the abject name of paganism, we must act
against it."

This, Richard, is why I hold faith in high esteem and hate reli-
gion. The first raises men up, the second drives them mad. Faith
is an intimate matter. And what is intimate, by definition, is not
a collective concern. Only religion decides that a profound and
secret personal belief must be taken from the heart and trans-
formed into a system of government. That is where the heresy
lies. When one decides a feeling must become a code of law.
Then, only religion can make atrocities appear to be good deeds.
Our descendants will come to know this at their peril. At pres-
ent, I grant you, this notion of jihad, despite its violence, is used
by men of honour. Educated and intelligent warriors, such as
were Zengi and Nur ad-Din, and as are their heirs, Saladin
and his brother Al-Adil. Of course, they make it a hypocritical
argument for conquest. But they fight man to man, and with

valour. The real danger will come when others take up this idea of jihad. They will hide in caves and boast of their courage. They won't even look into the eyes of their victims. As a general rule, madness is never born of a text, but of the person reading it. Saladin and his men know how to read. What will happen with the others?

But you cannot ignore the churches that also serve as mosques. Nor the Jewish, Muslim, and Christian quarters of Jerusalem!

Naïve child! Generosity is always an accident of history. Or the ruse of a pragmatic mind. Not something that will last very long. Religion only tolerates what is the same, wants what is identical. Another great difference with faith, which cares nothing for differences, since it is born in silence, in the depths of each soul, and flourishes outside the rules. Can't you see that by seeking to externalise what is intimate, religion imposes conformity? What is hidden should never be revealed to the light of day. Great things happen in the depths of our hearts, far from prying eyes. A time will come when everything must be spoken and shown. Then humankind will be lost, for, without a secret, man loses his strength.

Is that why you never show yourself? Why you give nothing, except orders? Why you venerate the words of the poets in order not to pronounce your own?

*

Months later, I will come to miss my mother. I will long for her as one longs for one's share of childhood, for I was never a little boy. Some of my lifetime will be amputated. In the space of an instant that will last for many nights, I, the king, will be one of the dispossessed, calling for my mother like one demands justice.

But before then, I will have made the most of our great reign. The victory of Saint John of Acre makes me the king of kings. Philip cannot bear it. He decides to abandon the cause and return to France. I take him down to the jetty, and we look at the ship. The sails seem to shiver slightly. He will have a safe crossing.

We have not spoken for a long time. But as we climb on deck, we exchange these explosive, catastrophic words. I play for frankness.

"You are afraid I will kill you. I will, if you touch Aquitaine."

He turns slowly towards me. He has grown thin, and cut his long blond hair. For me, there is nothing left of him but profound bitterness.

"You pushed me away from the manoeuvres and the fighting. I could only watch you in action, and lose the esteem of my men. I've also lost a sister, Alys, who should have been a queen but will forever remain a shadow, because of your rejection. It's not enough for you to win, Richard. You also have to humiliate me."

"Do not touch Aquitaine."

"You mean Eleanor of Aquitaine. Come now, you are king of England. Rest assured, I won't touch her."

In that moment, I know he is lying. And I feel ribbons of shadow rise up from my inner depths (where are they coming from? I was sure I had left them somewhere on a shoreline). They thicken and overflow until they darken the sky with a black haze which seems to hide a pair of eyes, ones I would swear were surrounded by a trace of opal, the green gaze of a king who was my father and confronted the grey gaze of my mother. Green against grey, marsh against armour, root against stormy sky, and me, me underneath it all, facing the approaching fog. It wraps around my sleep, stiffens my body in a dangerous rage and pours forth the image of my mother in chains after our defeat, locked in Salisbury tower, my mother on her lands, knowing she will be attacked, my mother who can sense and foresee events, and will obviously be able to defend herself, but my mother threatened by Philip. I forget the victory of Saint John of Acre and everything that makes me a noble man.

I turn on my heel.

For days, I let myself be invaded. When I reach the edge of the precipice, I gather up my men and order them to execute all the families of Saint John of Acre. I ignore their stupefaction, and for some, like Mercadier, their horrified stupefaction. There are husbands, wives, children, more than three thousand families, I know. This time I scream for these people to be brought to me and assassinated. I want these families dead.

As my men take their places in the city, the inhabitants observe us anxiously. The agreement I made with Saladin guarantees their safety. But on seeing my soldiers form ranks at all the strategic places of Saint John of Acre, they start to have doubts. The herbalists, the jewellers, the fruit-and-vegetable sellers pack up their stalls. The squares empty out. Only the awnings are waving gently in the warm air. A dog is playing with a pomegranate, nudging it with its nose, leaving a trail of red juice. I advance up a street of steps, all dust and silence, passing before doors barred with wooden planks. I choose a house at random. I smash down the door. I look for a bedroom, any bedroom. There is one on the first floor. I sit in a carved armchair, with armrests in the shape of serpents. I consider opening a large coffer inlaid with mother of pearl, then change my mind. Behind a white veil hanging from the ceiling, as if emerging from a light mist, I can make out a wide bed. A fine oval window, with wooden latticework above it, opens out onto a square where I have posted my men. I lean out. I give the signal for them to start.

The great killing begins. I stay seated in the bedroom, my sword on my knees. I caress it every once in a while. My back is to the window and the tumult reaches me. Crystalline screams, the shouts of men trying to resist, the silence of stabbed children. Slowly the ribbons of shadow grow thin and retreat. I am waiting for them to return to their lair. I wait for battle as one waits for a lover, the only place in the world where memory surrenders to action, where my sword and I decide over fate.

Fate arrives in the person of Mercadier, holding a roll of parchment, a message from Saladin, who has heard of the massacre. He has fixed the place for his revenge, a plain to the north of Arsuf, protected by forests that reach all the way down to the sea. I rise. It is time to live again. But Mercadier is moving too slowly not to attract my attention. I have seen him drunk, enraged, covered in blood, in armour, naked, falling over laughing, pressed against a girl, alone, but never like this. His little eyes tell of dizziness and exhaustion. Mercadier has just assassinated three thousand families.

"Only the men," he says breathlessly. "Punish me for not carrying out your orders. The women and children – I couldn't."

I squeeze his shoulder, which is larger than mine, and head for the terrace. Mercadier's voice resounds. Cavernous, a little hoarse, I know it well. But now, it breaks.

"Sire. I do not know what happened when Philip left, but you have been walking like a man who wants war and now you have provoked it. Saladin cannot remain impassive after what we have just done. You wanted a confrontation, you have just learned its location, but at what price? How can you live with these butchered children, these red walls? Blood is streaming through the streets."

I'll live very well, Mercadier. I'm used to it. I grew up with fury. I know how to push away the remorse it brings. I will advance holding my sword. As always. I will think of Eleanor's valour, and that will provoke the mix of anxiety and relief that is enough to keep me standing. On the battlefield, I will put the archers in the front line, before the knights. The Templars will be to the right, at the southern extremity, next to the Poitevin barons. I will be in the centre, with my English troops, and the Flemish behind me. To my left I will place the Knights Hospitaller. We will be there, in tight, squared-off ranks, behind our great almond-shaped shields emblazoned with the colours of our kingdoms. Saladin's attack will take place in the early morning, under a hard sun. He will send small squadrons, unrelentingly, that will tease the front lines of our archers, and then our knights. My tactic will be as follows: to stand our ground. Resist and reform the ranks as swiftly as possible. Saladin's squadrons will become aggressive, his provocations more frequent, with a few more men each time. They will charge at us with axes. They will try to get around the left flank of our army, the one most exposed to the plain. But on my orders, the Hospitallers will gather together after each assault. They will vacillate on their mounts, but keep clutching their hacked-up shields and immobile lances. I will feel the impatience of my soldiers, the enquiring looks of my barons. Some will argue, will shout out their doubts. I will not move. No one will understand that I am waiting for the Muslim army to approach as near as possible. For it to become imprudent. At that moment, I will raise my sword. I will call for the attack. The horses will spring forward. I will feel the army rise like a single body shaking itself off, a wave of colours and steel suddenly rushing forth. In the enemies' eyes we will see a brief spark of surprise. It will be so terrible and glorious that Saladin, high on his hill, will be able only to admire it.

And, of course, we will win.

There will be the morning, in the liquid light spreading over the harbour, when I contemplate my victory. It will be the most beautiful of all, with no delight and no hatred. A victory whose shape fits so closely with the world that it embeds itself into it, naturally, never to be moved.

For three days, Hakim cares for the injured, whispering soft words, moving gently, repairing limbs, sewing up wounds. He saves more men than all the camp doctors put together. He seems exhausted. He knows we will be marching on Jerusalem to take it back from Saladin. That will be another great battle, this time more violent than any we have ever known. Hakim asks to speak to me. I see a withered man coming towards me, majestic despite his soiled tunic. He sits on a coffer. His hands flat on his thighs, he speaks very softly, looking at the ground:

"Sire. You are going to fight for Jerusalem. If you win, I will have betrayed my people, and this victory will taste so bitter that I will no longer be able to live. If you lose, my people will kill me. I am done for. You can therefore ask me anything you wish."

So I spend a long night with Hakim, discussing our differences. He answers politely, patiently. I couldn't care less about converting him. I love the East too much not to be interested in its beliefs. Our exchange is so fruitful that I think, several times, I should memorise it and write it down for my mother. Hakim tells me how shocked he is by our loose morals and our cruelty, and cannot allow that the son of God could have been born of a woman. I counter with the polygamy here, and whether cutting off one's enemies' heads is not a form of cruelty, and ask him where, in his opinion, men and gods come from, if not from between women's thighs? He grows silent, then our discussion starts up again. When I tell him that in my country the cathedrals are full of colour and people from morning until night, that they serve as meeting places and markets full of selling and singing, his surprise is such that I cannot but laugh. I explain that, along with cemeteries and public squares, these are the three areas that are freely accessible in an occidental city. Despite his pained look, I tell him about the celebrations among the tombstones.

In the morning, we are standing in the dust, among the knights coming out of the tents and shaking themselves awake in the sunshine. Hakim takes my hand and talks to me in his language. He pauses from time to time, looks at the horizon, and starts again. It sounds like a promise. I don't understand what he is saying, but his voice is shaking. I let him talk. In the end, he kisses my hand.

My son. I am writing this letter to you from the priory of Hereford, as a matter of urgency. I hope it will reach you before it is too late. You must come home. I put your delay on the count of the cold season. You let it pass and you were right to do so. Winter in the East is muddy, I remember it well, and rain is never favourable for long journeys. But now, you have no more excuses. John and Philip have allied themselves against us. They have announced that you will not come home. On December 25, they met, with their vassals, at Fontainebleau. Quite a Christmas present . . . They want to invade England, and steal your crown. Then they will aim for Aquitaine.

I try not to cut off the connection with John. It is becoming more and more difficult. He knows that there is no heir to stand in his way, since Berengaria is not pregnant. Come home, Richard. You are king of England and duke of Aquitaine. Come home, or we will lose everything.

I lower the letter. My lips are dry. The wind is beating at the nape of my neck with the implacability of a young master. And then there are the pebbles under my feet, the same impervious nature as in Aquitaine. I understand it now, journeys don't take one very far.

My Eleanor is worried, and that is so unlike her. But she is insightful, as always. It hasn't escaped her that here, at war, I am at last at peace.

So Philip lied to me, just as I foresaw it. He and John want to take my kingdom, my throne, and my mother's peace of mind. She will have fought unstintingly to achieve what she knows how to do best, reign. I am the duke of Aquitaine and king of England. Who dares to attack the one who bore and raised me? Who dares to reveal her to me as fragile? My anger rises, it is my mother's caress. The memories pour in. The attack is so sudden that I feel a slight dizziness. Here, in a fog, is Eleanor pointing out a field to me, telling me the history of her Poitou; her cheeks are pink after a gallop; I'm thirteen years old, my heart swollen with pride. Here are the poets that make Matilda blush. And here, the smell of the great ducal hall, a smell of cold embers and reeds, or the scent of lilies perfuming our chambers, or of amber as Eleanor sat at William's deathbed. Here she is at her wedding with my father, in a red gown, with threads of gold woven into her hair, my mother to whom no one would ever show disrespect.

And so my ghosts emerge slowly, my brothers and sisters, united in the certainty that such a heinous deed must be punished. It is not just about Eleanor, they whisper, since we are here too. We are all walking behind her. I fold the letter. The intent of the battle now before us will be to wash away an insult. It will be Jerusalem. I am attacking the most coveted, punishing target, for this battle must be an arduous one. But, in the end, the enemy or the city do not matter. I will be the only one to know what I am putting into this. I will be the only one to know that, behind each blow, there will be the respect of the oath: "Raise up what is destroyed, preserve what is standing."

The Lament of the Forsaken Bride

RICHARD, AS YOU READY YOURSELF *for a colossal battle, you don't spare a single thought for me. And yet, I was your betrothed. Do you remember me? Alys, a shadow in your history, a ghost who is not one of your retinue. Your absent companions know nothing of me. Even the poets did not consider my story worthy of interest. I leave no trace. And yet, I am the daughter of Louis VII, the king of France. And I was meant to be your wife. I have no place in your life, I represent nothing. I am a princess, chosen for you, who are now the king of England, and I do not exist. Because one evening after a banquet, when I was twelve years old, your father followed me into my bedchamber, and quite naturally, with no brutality, laid me down on the bed. I did not scream — no one resisted the Plantagenet. Your father's repugnant act spread throughout the kingdom. The Church said nothing, nor did my family, and you, my future husband, barred me from your life. No one ever talked about it openly, as if the crime had never taken place.*

That evening, after your father's departure, I pulled down my dress and called my servants for the bedtime ritual. And I never slept in a bed again. You certainly know this, for I was ridiculed for it: I am the one who sets out a fur blanket at the foot of my bed, and who sleeps there, on the ground. Sometimes, when the memory of your father's gasping breath is too loud, I pull on a cape, take a candle, and leave the sleeping castle. I look for a lime tree — that beneficent tree planted near leprosy hospitals because it gives honey, its bark is pliable, and its wood is soft — and lie down under the branches, on the ground, to wait until rest comes. No one will come here to turn my body over, or my life upside down.

I waited for you to avenge me. But the revolt you started against the Plantagenet was not about me at all. You attacked my assailant, not because of your love for me, but for the love of your mother. I feel no bitterness about this. That would be absurd — Eleanor is so far above me. I was imprisoned with her in the tower at Salisbury, I remember it well . . . A single gesture from her, and I would turn to stone. She has the power to transfix others. And also the stinging repartee that is the mark of great reserve. It's not hard to imagine . . . How could I rival her? I am one of those women who prepare a sage bath, keep an eye on the kitchens, listen for a returning gallop. I am someone to care for a husband, not to launch an offensive against him. Ogres devour women like me. Standing up to the Plantagenet, and occupying your heart, requires a woman of Eleanor's tempering. I was defeated, right from the start. But I also feel gratitude for these queens. One should know how to admire what one does not possess.

The only thing I am afraid of is that your love for Eleanor might damage you in the end. One can lose oneself by searching too long for a look. And her eyes are armour, defending for fear of giving.

I have seen you collect exploits, surpass your limits, launch the unthinkable attack against your father. You always want more, and now, again, after Saint John of Acre, you want Jerusalem. I have watched you advance alone, always so alone, and I know that behind those excesses, whether sorrowful or grandiose, hiding somewhere, is the mad terror that your mother might turn away from you.

Beware of expectations, Richard, and protect yourself from Eleanor's grey eyes.

If I am telling you all this, it is because, on the eve of your great battle, I would like to offer you what courage is left in me. To offer you a little valour, despite my soiled body and my sad childhood in the palace in Île-de-France. Today I am a recluse in a small château in France, surrounded by lime trees. I sew, and look after my potager. I visit the peasants, I help the needy. My memories of you, of what might have been if you had married me, keep me company. I am not the kind of woman to talk about myself; but sometimes, floating behind the present moment, I see the glimmering of my past. It is set like a stone in water, at the bottom of my life, giving the surface a particular colour. Sorrows are not a burden. They soften my existence with a peaceful, *velvety shadow. I have no glory and no prestige to offer you, and I would have so loved to be at your side in the East. But the resignation that fills my life today is also an obstinate power. And so I see you by the fire, reading your mother's letter, and I take my place in your shared story. I send you my regrets, for that is all I have, and my renunciation, in hopes that their tenacity will help you. The battle before you will be bloody. You may lose your life. This is the last wish of a prisoner, whom you alone might have lifted up from the ground and laid in a bed: that all my sorrows be with you.*

FOR WEEKS NOW, WE HAVE been circling Jerusalem. It stands in a landscape of bare hills, parched by the sun, from where I can admire the carpet of ochre roofs, the sacred sites, and especially the top of David's citadel, where water and grain are stocked – a warrior never has the eyes of a believer, he only sees strategic points. High walls protect this city that used to belong to us, and which Saladin has taken back.

I have dispersed my army into little groups. Each one must take a citadel near by. My men have attacked and taken Jaffa, blocked the road to Caesarea, and invited themselves into a caravanserai waiting for supplies for Jerusalem. The moment the convoy passed through the high vaulted gates, my men jumped down from the stairs, rose up from the terraces. They looted everything. Now we have food, water, and new horses.

However, I commit an error. I am late in assembling my whole army for the final assault. When I understand my mistake, I immediately call back my men. But the soldiers are further away than planned. They will take time to reach me.

Which means that if Saladin attacks, I will not have all my troops around me.

He knows this. He is getting organised. He has obtained reinforcements from Mosul and galvanised his troops. He has cut down all the fruit trees at the foot of the walls, filled all the wells.

Saladin chooses dawn, the hour when vigilance slackens, carried away by the long watches of the night. Mercadier, whose sleep is as light as his body is large, is the first to open his eyes. The pink sky, the blue light of darkness, then the neighing of horses and the flashing of steel in the rising sun; he is up like a lightning bolt. He screams my name. I leap up. My sword is on me, as always. My men are not as fast and grab what they have to hand. I can hear the tramping of the enemy army behind the hills. There are more than five thousand of them. At a glance, I measure my mistake. I have fifty-two armed knights, fifteen horses at the ready, and two thousand foot soldiers.

I may die here, without saving Eleanor. A mad idea comes to me. I order a long palisade to be built with the tent poles. Behind it, I arrange my soldiers in pairs, with their shields in front of them and two lances in their hands. When Saladin's horses jump the palisade, they must raise their lances to spear them in the belly.

Between each pair of soldiers, I post an archer. The objective is not to attack, for we are too few, but to repel. On my destrier, as the enemy cavalcade approaches, I harangue my troops. My voice carries far beyond the hills. I brandish my royal coat of arms. I remind them of their commitment to the land, their knights' oaths — "Thou shalt love the country of thy birth" — and at these words, hands grip hilts. I repeat my instructions: under no circumstances launch an attack, but merely hold firm, close the ranks, to the glory of the sword, our only family.

The moment I pronounce these words, Saladin attacks. The first three charges are of a thousand men each. I order the archers to the front lines. Their arrows are made of poisonous yew wood, those trees planted in cemeteries, propagating death. My archers shoot and retreat. Then the first enemy horses jump over the palisade, the lances rise and open their bellies. Terrible neighing, haloes of dust around turban cloths, then my soldiers take up their lances again and wait for the next attack.

At Saladin's fourth attack, I am in the first line to push back his men. I am a rampart, even if I have never been able to protect what is most important. I achieve in war what I was never able to achieve in life. The threat floating over Eleanor, the memory of my dismembered family lifts me up and pushes me into a fearsome rage. At the enemy's seventh charge, my shield is nothing but a pile of wood, and my steed is exhausted. Without fear, I advance into the fray. My best knights follow me. We have become a barrage of shouting men, of swirling swords. The limbs of our enemies fly around us, our trained destriers know when to rear. Behind us, my archers are shooting relentlessly. My foot soldiers continue to raise their lances the instant the enemy horses jump. The animals, slashed open and half lying on the poles, offer further protection. The Saracens are finished off and my soldiers recover their weapons. Quite soon, they have one in each hand. Our wall of dead horses is holding.

At the front, we are slaying like devils. I first aim for the heads. Then comes the moment when my steed collapses, wounded in the leg. I get out of the saddle, quickly, and leap into a combat position. A moment later, I can just make out a figure advancing with a superb, barely frightened stallion. He's an equerry. What is he doing here? His turban is soaked in blood. He walks with shaky steps, avoiding blows, trying to make his way through the war. It's a miracle that he reaches me. I grasp the reins. A gift from Saladin, the groom indicates, before crumpling to the ground. Saladin, somewhere in the battle, or perched on a hill, has ordered a fresh mount to be given to me.

Mercadier's horse has been injured too. He has dismounted. He swivels around. With one hand, he yanks out his sword from a torso, and with the other, he bursts a skull with his fist. He can sense the next blow – anticipation, the mark of a great warrior. We are sloshing around in a mixture of mud and blood. We are roaring beasts, our hackles raised by instinct. My new steed turns like a crazed spinning top. I can sense who is going to strike and where. My fist holds firm to my sword as it plunges ceaselessly into throats. The hours pass and my men are ceaselessly killing, while at the rear, they are pushing back. A few enemies manage to get over the palisade. My barons have posted men to slice the forelocks of the horses and finish off the imprudent soldiers. War cries finish in hiccups. My name and the name of our kingdom resound everywhere. Mercadier calls out my name, but his voice trembles in warning. The instant I turn to him, I see the blade of a dagger ready to kill me. Mercadier lunges onto the man and stabs his back. He stands up again, holding the convulsing body by the neck. He holds it out to me. I recognise Hakim.

The day draws to an end. The air freshens. We are still in a fury. Mercadier has seized an axe. The horses slip over the bodies. Less energy, of course, but just as much rancour. How long have we been fighting? I don't know anymore. Never have I held my sword in this way. It is my hand, my skin, a part of me. While my mother always stands to one side of things, ready to defy but never to welcome them, I am in among them, completely. The battle offers me the present moment, with no hesitation or half-measures. It offers the memory of my father — for my father, as opposed to my mother, could not detach himself from base emotion, could never stand far enough back from events for them not to make him their plaything, crush him as they wished, crumple and throw him to the ground — how else to explain his exploding anger, of which I was ashamed for so long? And so, yes, I get that from him too, but this similarity is what saves me on the battlefield — it is my best ally. Do not take umbrage, Mother, but in order to slash two men at once, to keep one's ears open, to stab with the speed of an eagle, you need to be impulsive, unthinking, selfish – to be a Plantagenet. And I am. On the battlefield I am the son of my father alone. Forgive me, Mother, war is my declaration of independence from you. My sword protests against the love I bear you, and takes my side, declaring my freedom.

I am making sure the palisade is still valiantly defended when suddenly, unexpectedly, the voice of one of Saladin's commanders comes down from the sky. A powerful, hoarse voice, carrying over this hell, and whose intention we immediately understand.

Retreat.

Then the enemies suddenly rein around. Those still fighting man to man can hope to have their lives spared. Some of the wounded start crawling towards the hills. Others struggle away, then fall to the ground. We remain stunned, breathless, our blades still at the ready. It seems to last an eternity. Then Mercadier turns towards me. He lifts up his great helm. On his face, spattered with blood, a wide smile appears.

I hardly dare to believe it. My men advance, haggardly; some fall to their knees. I lean against the flank of a dead horse and have the feeling I am just like it. Exhaustion falls on me like a cast-iron trap. I stand there, looking at the ground, panting. My feet are stuck in a red and ochre sludge, constellated with dark, thick patches. The earth after a battle. My banner has been planted there with an unhurried movement.

The breeze gently unfurls the cloth, showing the gold lion against the rosy sky. I raise my head. Laughter peals, first timidly, then louder, then as a booming consort. No one has the strength to stand anymore. So they hiccup, their heads between their legs; they fall to the ground, roll on the bodies, lie on their backs, palms open, laughing and crying all at once, their heads thrown back under the moon.

Hidden in my tunic, on my chest shuddering with exhausted laughter, is Eleanor's letter.

It is time to sort the bodies. Ours will be buried. With a thrust of his chin, Mercadier points out Hakim to me. He is lying with a gash on his back, his head in the mud. I think of the last time he spoke to me, his hand in mine. His voice was trembling with gratitude.

"Perhaps not, sire," says Mercadier. "Perhaps he was warning you he was going to kill you."

I look down at his hand, lying half open. If Mercadier is right, then Hakim was a man of his word. He will be buried with our men.

Now I need to announce my decision. I must confront the fury of my men. We will not occupy Jerusalem. We are going home.

"Going home? But, sire! Jerusalem is right here! What was the point of what we just accomplished?"

I was expecting this. I face them. My barons are beside themselves. I have just explained to them that if we occupy

Jerusalem, there will be no one to be her king. Their disappointment is even stronger. They reproach me for not attempting it. I try to respond calmly. To resist my first impulse, which would be to send them all to the devil and call for departure. I try to steady my voice:

"We can enter Jerusalem, that's true. And then what? Who will govern it? None of you here are the stuff of kings. Take the holy city only to let it get away from us again? I prefer to negotiate with Saladin."

Cries of indignation ring out. I hear that I am sold to the enemy, that Saladin has more influence on me than my own camp. Some of the men who fought with me during the revolt against my father even call out that defamatory nickname: "Oc e no". I get to my feet and walk away.

Later, in my tent, Mercadier serves me some wine. When he puts the jug down, I'm afraid he might have broken it. And yet I know that he has just made a monumental effort to move softly.

"Without wishing to misreckon, sire. And just for my own knowledge. Is Queen Eleanor perhaps in danger?"

She is. And now that I have made war with my past, now that I am victorious, she will have the best of me to defend her.

But I do not say any of that. My cup crosses the tent and hits Mercadier's forehead. He does not attempt even the slightest evasive movement. And while a line of blood slowly trickles down his face, he bows, impassively, and turns away.

*

September 2, 1192, Saladin's emissary stands before me, with an offer: peace for five years; the coastal cities restored to the Christians; free access for Christians to the holy sites of Jeru-salem. The sketch of a temporary cohabitation between Christians and Muslims. Thus, the old adage was confirmed: "He who wants peace prepares for war" — a saying that others, in future times, will judge to be barbaric. The emissary then points to crates of peaches, pears, and melted snow from Mount Hermon, "to cool your drinks", he says. "This gift is intended for Queen Eleanor, your mother."

When the arrow from a crossbow pierces my shoulder, on March 29, 1199, long after my return, that is the first thing to cross my mind: I will never drink the snow from Mount Her-mon. I will never see those mountains, as white as Matilda's skin, or breathe that dry dust again. Then I feel like laughing. What an irony! Having known those eastern landscapes, defied my father, beaten Saladin, only to die of an arrow wound, dur-ing a routine siege in Limousin! Mercadier's desperate cry is what makes me open my eyes. Then I think of her.

On my return from the crusade, I was captured by the king of Austria, who demanded an exorbitant ransom. The equivalent of two years of revenues to the English crown . . . For a year, my mother rode throughout all of Europe to collect that fortune. She succeeded. I was set free. And so when I feel myself being lifted off the ground, I tell myself that if my mother managed to amass that ransom then, surely she will find a way for me to survive now. The naïvety of the dying! And as my head rolls against Mercadier's shoulder, I think of the abbey of Fontevraud, for I would like to be buried there too, beneath the white powdery arches. I mumble my wishes against Mercadier's ear, who seems to understand, from the way he nods his head like a crazed puppet. My eyelids are heavy. I am set down on the ground. I wonder what she will feel when she learns of my death. Will she suffer? Will I be the only crack in that rampart of a mother? Did she love me even a little? That question comes to mind just as the arrow is pulled out, and maybe that is not a coincidence: my feelings for Eleanor are always mixed with pain, after all. As they cut my tunic off me, I can see the future, clearly, and if I appear to struggle in Mercadier's arms, it is not because of the wound, but because I would like to warn my mother, to tell her to stop everything now, because Philip will win. On all fronts. He will sprinkle his castles all over France, impose their architec-ture. He will attack my magnificent Château-Gaillard. My ship, my stone treasure! He will make it a point of honour to conquer it. The inhabitants will call my brother John to their aid. He will lift his head briefly from his chess game, in Eng-land, and say, "Do whatever seems best."

My fortress will be taken after eight months of battle. In the same movement, Philip will march on Aquitaine. He will set fire to our forests. On August 10, 1204, he will enter Poitiers. It will be over, there will be nothing left of our kingdom. But no matter. By that date, my mother will be no more. She will be resting in Fontevraud, in that tranquillity she never knew. By my side. She will be sculpted lying with her feet pointing towards the East. Her statue will rest there, under the radiant light of the vaults. Nature, so beloved and so incriminated, will breathe all around her. For I understand this as I am dying: what I took for indifference was, in fact, a majestic fidelity. And I, the ignorant one seeing only my own troubles, never understood that nature abandons no one. Like the sword. Like my mother. Between her sculpted hands, an open book will be placed, with blank pages. "This life that was all journeys and wars", the poets will say at her death. I am leaving with books left to write. For I would like the story of Eleanor to be written, of the woman who wished to be king, who failed, and then became much more. The mother who said nothing, but whose actions revealed so much. The child who bore children, and buried them. The woman I was not able to console. I would like to write the story of all mothers who did their best, with worried pride, feeling sure that they would conquer tragedies. My lips move and Mercadier leans towards me, grimacing in sadness, trying to catch my words. Maybe he will recognise my birth song. This poem, which says as much about Eleanor as it does about me, I'll try to sing it so I won't die alone, so I can die a little closer to her.

The many mishaps, the many obstacles
Did not defeat him.
Nor the crashing seas, nor their terrible wrath,

Nor the depths of the valley, nor the lofty summits,
Nor the daring heights, nor the rocky roads,
Nor the beaten track with its winding lines,
Nor the inviolate desert, nor the angry wind,
Nor the clouds, drunk with their colossal flows,
Nor the terrible storm streaming down . . .

Author's note

THIS NOVEL, BY DEFINITION, IS not a history book.
It recounts the times of Richard the Lionheart, as seen
from his standpoint, and with the diffractions created by the
prism of his experience.

I used an established historical outline, but I also took certain liberties. For example, the fleur-de-lys on the royal banner
was not a decision made by Louis VII; there was not yet a
keep at Dover; the motto "Raise up what is destroyed, preserve what is standing" was not an oath of Richard the
Lionheart's; the word "crusade" did not exist in the Middle
Ages . . .

On the other hand, some elements are taken from historical works. Richard's battles in the East are authentic; the
word "jihad" was used by Saladin; the Plantagenet's rages,
the storm at Barfleur when Eleanor was pregnant, the story
of William, of Alys, and of Rosamund Clifford, as well as
the songs and extracts of letters cited, none of these are
invented . . .

One could amuse oneself by listing what is imaginary and

what is real. However, it is essential not to make the mistake of opposing the workings of the novel to that of the historian, since they complement each other so well.

Clara Dupont-Monod

Acknowledgments

To Olivier Roller.
To Martin Aurell and Manuel Carcassonne.

CLARA DUPONT-MONOD studied ancient French at the Sorbonne, and began her career in journalism writing for *Cosmopolitan* and *Marianne*. Her novels often draw on medieval myths and history, and have been nominated for the Prix Goncourt and the Prix Femina, two of France's most prestigious literary awards. She lives in Paris, and has been haunted by the story of Eleanor of Aquitaine for many years. *The Revolt* is her first novel to appear in English translation.

RUTH DIVER is the winner of the 2016 *Asymptote* Close Approximations Fiction Prize for her translation of *Maraudes* by Sophie Pujas. She was the Head of Comparative Literature at the University of Auckland until 2014. Her first full-length translation was Adélaïde Bon's *The Little Girl on the Ice Floe* in 2019; *The Revolt* is her second.

Help us make the next generation of readers

We all – author, translator and publisher – hope you enjoyed this book.
We believe that you can become a reader at any time in your life,
but we'd love your help to give the next generation a head start.

Did you know that 9% of children don't have a book of their
own in their home, rising to 13% in disadvantaged families*?
We'd like to try to change that by asking you to consider the role
you could play in helping to build readers of the future.

We'd love you to think of sharing, borrowing, reading, buying or talking
about a book with a child in your life and spreading the love of reading.
We want to make sure the next generation continue to have access
to books, wherever they come from.

And if you would like to consider donating to charities that help
fund literacy projects, find out more at www.literacytrust.org.uk
and www.booktrust.org.uk.

Thank you.

*As reported by the National Literacy Trust